I0730111

WORMWOOD ABBEY

THE SECRETS OF ORMDALE
BOOK ONE

CHRISTINA BAEHR

Copyright © 2023 by Christina Baehr

All rights reserved.

No part of this publication may be reproduced, distributed, or transmitted in any form or by any means, including photocopying, recording, or other electronic or mechanical methods, without the prior written permission of the publisher. For permission requests, contact books@christinabaehr.com

The story, all names, characters, and incidents portrayed in this production are fictitious.

Cover Illustration and Design by Shiloh Longbottom

To my nine dragons, who have been known to bite.

I will sit still and let the marvels and the adventures settle on me like flies. There are plenty of them, I assure you. The world will never starve for want of wonders; but only for want of wonder.

— G.K. Chesterton, *Tremendous Trifles* (1909)

CHAPTER ONE

"Wormwood Abbey?" I read aloud the address of the sender of a letter directed to my father, the Reverend G. E. Worms. "What a ridiculous name!" I exclaimed, referring to the name of the Abbey.

Worms was also a ridiculous name, but after twenty-one years of life I had got used to it.

My father looked up, slightly startled, from his newspaper. "What did you say, Edith? But that must be from my people."

Mother also looked up, from her new issue of *The Parents' Review (April, 1899)*. She took the unopened letter from me and passed it across the breakfast table to Father. The *Review* she quietly laid on the table. Things were pretty serious if she did that.

The three of us—Mother, George, and I—were very grave as Father read it.

Father very seldom spoke of his family. They had disowned him when he married my mother, his first wife. Nor was their silence broken or any help offered to him at all when she died during my infancy and left my father to raise me alone.

George, who at eleven years of age could not be expected to be grave for very long, broke in with: "Sir, is that where you saw the dragon?"

Mother shook her head and I stopped George's questions with an unexpected second helping from the jam pot, of which I had been appointed guardian.

I had the exact same thought as George. Our father, a warm, communicative man, had remained singularly uncommunicative on the subject of his childhood.

The bare outline we knew: sent away from his country home to a school where cruelty went unpunished. My father was an imaginative child, and his flights of fancy were interpreted as lying and met with merciless beatings from tutors and schoolfellows alike. This culminated in a pathetic attempt to run away to sea—perhaps it was telling that he thought the Queen's Navy would be an improvement on his circumstances. In response, Father was removed from school and privately tutored, boarding at his tutor's house until he was ready to go up to Oxford to study Divinity.

Stories of his childhood were very few, but one in particular was well known to both of us.

"When I was a child, I saw a dragon in the garden," he would say, in a soft voice, taking us with him to a summer twilight at his family's remote seat in Yorkshire. (No doubt this was just the kind of story that had found an unappreciative audience in his schoolfellows.)

The 'dragon' had been about the size of an Alpine Mastiff, the kind that rescue hapless day-trippers that lose themselves in the Swiss alps. I was convinced that the companion of that happy moment had been such a dog, in very fact.

Our little family was now settled in the thriving parish of St Giles in a very civilised East Midlands town, and as far as I was concerned we had shaken the dust of Yorkshire from our feet, never to return. Not that I'd ever actually been there to get its dust on my feet, for which I had no regrets.

Father put the letter down shakily. "I think I'd like a cup of tea now."

"Is it bad news, dear?" Mother queried as she poured out. Since stepmothers are always either horrible or angelic in stories, I might as well tell you at once that mine is firmly in the latter category. She is every inch the angel she looks.

Father was staring at the marmalade as if it was the ghost of marmalades past and didn't answer for a moment.

"They—they want us to have it."

"Have what?"

"It. The Abbey."

Mother and I looked at one another in dismay. George threw his cap in the air.

"Hoorah!"

THE PLAN WAS SOON MADE and put into motion. The train journey would take the better part of the day. We would go to the very end of the railway line, into the utter wilds of that network of valleys and upland moors known as the Yorkshire Dales. We would make this journey hoping that we would be met with a conveyance to take us to the Abbey, as the letter had promised.

When one is a clergyman's daughter in a busy city parish like me, one always has mourning garb that fits. There are always parishioners to mourn and funerals to attend. At present the people whom we were supposed to be mourning were my uncle (father's elder brother, Cadmus) and his son (Percy, my first cousin). The irony of dressing in mourning for people who would never have done so for us was not lost on me.

As I arranged myself in a first class train carriage with my family, I felt, more than anything, irritated at my unknown cousin and uncle for dying so dramatically (a 'hunting accident,' the letter informed us) and at such an inconvenient time.

Over the last two years I had had some success publishing detective stories under a pseudonym. I was currently writing to a deadline from my publisher. My informal duties as clergyman's daughter had kept me busy as we completed Lent and entered Eastertide. I could not afford many more days away from my writing desk without suffering for it.

"Fancy a bit of blood and thunder for the trip, Edith?" said Father, with an eyebrow arched towards the racks of yellow-backed novels on the platform. It was a joke he loved; the fact that my own novels were among those on the racks was a secret known to very few.

"Father, you know I always bring something sensational to read on the train," I replied, tapping the thick notebook in my lap which contained notes for the next Inspector Green mystery.

Hours later, the train stopped at a station as we were passing from Lancashire into Yorkshire. Looking out the window I chanced to notice the elaborate ironwork supporting the platform canopy above. At the centre of the circular design of Lancaster roses there crouched a fierce winged beast with a barbed tail, the precise name of which escaped me. For some reason, it interested me. It had the tail of a dragon and the wings of a pegasus, and its belly was low to the ground.

As the train pulled away, I turned to Father, who could always be counted on to know such things. "Father, what's the name of that creature that's always appearing on heraldry? The one with the rather upset expression?"

"Two legs or four?" asked Father.

"Two."

"A wyvern, my dear."

"Perhaps that was the creature you saw in the garden. They seem to be fond of them in these parts." I checked my watch. "Father, please tell us what we should know about these people. We hardly know anything about them, and I've no wish to disgrace you upon the occasion of our entering the ranks of the Landed Gentry."

My tone was slightly tart. Father suddenly looked wearied. I regretted the tartness at once. I might scoff at 'these people,' but they were the only family my father had ever known, as callous as they had been towards him.

"Edith, I wish I knew what to say. I haven't laid eyes on my family since I was nine years old. As I understand it, brother has—had—four children. The surviving ones are all daughters, unknown to me. God knows I have no desire to deprive my nieces of their home."

"Of course not, dear." Mother squeezed his arm. "What a trying time it must be for them."

Mother is the perfect clergyman's wife, always ready with tea, jars of calf's foot jelly, infant stockings, and tactful words. Characteristically, she did not think of mentioning what a trying time it was for *us*.

"I'm sure there must be something we can do to put an end to this nonsense," I said, not for the first time.

I like to think I am not at all bad at being a clergyman's daughter, though I am not as dab a hand at the clerical life as Mother. With my square face and small, tidy figure I'm a picture of feminine rectitude. My springy hair is the only thing that hints at wilder proclivities. It is usually tamped down with a hat. I dress myself neatly and well but without ostentation, and I know how to keep my mouth shut when I have any thoughts that might cause shock or dismay.

For most of the year, I get away with a few trite aphorisms after the service or at tea with the parishioners and then—bliss!—I'm off to my study to write.

Everyone thinks I'm making some sort of translation because it got about that Father taught me Greek years ago (he tried). This is very convenient. I'm sure people would not be half so respectful if they knew I was writing about damsels in distress and poisons and police inspectors. I make sure to pepper my conversation every now and then with barely relevant references to Lady Julian of Norwich or the Venerable Bede or Boethius, just often enough to keep up this valuable misapprehension.

To MY RELIEF, there was indeed a carriage with an aged retainer to meet us at Embsay station, which appeared to be not only the end of the line but also of civilisation. From the desolation of the last part of our journey I had half expected to be abandoned at the station and forced to cadge a ride on some agricultural equipage.

I could just imagine us arriving at the ancestral seat, picking bits of hay from our mourning costumes, or perhaps drenched to the skin with rain from our journey over the lowering moor. Perhaps the wind would even wuther at us for good measure. What a way to announce ourselves!

But no, we were respectably met, and the spring day was only a little grey. I detected no wuthering, whatever that might be, precisely.

What a strange sensation to enter that carriage! It was

my first contact with something that belonged to my father's family. My own experience of life was so much of the middle class. Carriages, for me, were something one hired and did not own. Did this carriage, even now, belong to my father? Was it in some sense my own?

I did not feel any richer by it. If anything, I felt a little burdened. Though it seemed well-kept on the whole, with a patina of age and a scent of polish, the upholstery was obviously threadbare in places. Owning such things must surely bring more trouble than convenience.

Some time later we passed through a very small village composed of poor stone cottages which Father said was Ormdale village, and in some way associated with the Estate. After that it was miles of open land, threaded with an ancient rock boundary wall, about waist high. It was a mute and dogged companion on our journey, and, besides the rough road, the only sign of civilisation on this wild and endless landscape.

Presently the narrow road drew close to the bank of the river. My father looked out of the window with an expression of dawning recognition. George by this time was pretty much hanging out of it with eagerness.

We now entered a valley with sloping sides that showed white here and there with limestone. The river was taking us in.

Now we passed into a wood. I was struck with how profound was the secrecy of this place. I felt for a moment that we were passing from a country to which I belonged (wilder than the England I knew but still recognisable) into somewhere absolutely unknown, a place where R.D. Blackmore's outlaws might have hidden undetected for centuries more.

I felt my heartbeat quicken. Despite myself, I was

growing more and more alive to the excitement of the journey.

The road climbed steeply for a time and we were fairly jostled. Now the trees thinned and the countryside opened suddenly like a book falling open on its spine. Father quickly turned his head, as if following some forgotten childhood habit, to look out of the other side of the carriage. We all followed suit.

At first sight, I thought it a ruin. One wing was ruined indeed, and the high pointed windows showed us again the wide grey Yorkshire sky.

Then I saw smoke rising from Tudor chimneys. This was no ghostly relic. This was my own family's ancient home, whether we sought it or not.

The carriage slowed as we approached. George jumped out before we could stop him and ran alongside. Soon the carriage pulled up outside of the inhabited wing of the building. I saw Mother slip her hand into Father's. Father did look a bit green, poor dear.

We extracted ourselves. A group of people were standing near the front door to meet us. George arrived first and skidded to a halt, suddenly at a loss.

There were three young females in deep mourning. Naturally, I noticed the oldest first, who was about my own age. Tall and willowy, her eyes large and expressive, her dark hair lustrous, she looked just like what she was: a beautiful creature brought about by centuries of careful breeding. Her fine features had an air of courage and silent suffering. She looked like the kind of heroines I invented for my own novels. I invented them because they were everything I could never be.

My father took her hand in his. "You must be my niece, Gwendolyn. How I wish we could have met in happier times. This is my daughter, Edith."

Gwendolyn nodded, barely glancing at me, and gestured to the other two. "These are my sisters, Violet and Una."

I swallowed my humiliation at being completely overlooked by my eldest cousin and turned to my younger ones. Violet was, incongruously, smiling brightly, as if she was in quite a different story than the rest of us. She was a sturdy, well-grown girl with brown hair, and had reached her teens without any of the timidity which can afflict girls of this age. Violet was an absurd name for her.

"Hello, Uncle George, Cousin Edith." She stepped up to me and took my hand. It warmed me after Gwendolyn's chill.

Our final cousin, light-haired Una, looked like an illustration from a child's book of prayers, the ones with pious and apparently mindless children that have to have angels hovering over them to stop them tumbling off cliffs.

Father introduced me and Mother and drew George into the group. "This is your cousin George. He must be about your age." He looked at Una. "I hope you will be great friends."

I do wish people would not say this. It is never an inducement to friendship and it is often an impediment. In this case, Una startled like a skittery foal. She looked up at Gwendolyn for reassurance. Gwendolyn responded with a firm but unreadable glance. Una remembered her manners and wafted a sad, saintly smile in George's general direction. George's eyelid twitched.

I felt quite sure that any great friendship between these two would be very hard won. Between myself and Gwendolyn, I judged, there was no possibility of it. She had quickly made it clear that I was insignificant to her.

Gwendolyn led us inside. We passed through a Tudor portico that must have been added on to the original

Abbey. It was carved—writhing with toothy, tailed figures —but I did not have time to examine the carvings then, as Violet was tugging me inside.

Now we were in a great hall with a large staircase and fireplace. There was no fire, but there was a large oaken settle near the hearth, which looked small in the enormous room. There were dimly coloured tapestries which I longed to admire more closely but I felt that I must not gape as if I had paid a shilling to see the house.

A realisation came to me with an unwelcome jolt: I cared what these people thought of me. It was a feeling I did not enjoy.

I had no leisure to gape at any rate as Gwendolyn had efficiently disentangled Violet from me and was taking Mother and me upstairs to take off our things.

We followed up the great staircase to a passage with several rooms. We went inside one and found it surprisingly comfortable. There was a fire here, and warm water in a pitcher. I had seen no servants so far, but this was evidence that they existed.

In front of washstand and mirror, I unpinned my hat reluctantly. I always feel much more impressive with a hat. My hair is my worst point. It is a light red, and the texture of cotton wool. At its worst it looks like the hair of an ill-behaved fairy. Mother calls it auburn but it is nothing of the kind. I have always suspected I inherited it from my real mother's side of the family. It is not a Patrician colour.

I felt at this moment that it marked me as low-born and out of place in this atmosphere of ancient privilege. I felt a pang of shame, and then a burn of resentment against this family that made me feel shame where I ought to feel none.

I tensed my already firm jaw and lifted my eyes to meet Gwendolyn's. She was, to my surprise, gazing at me with a curious kind of intensity. At the moment of our meeting I had felt dismissed by her. What had happened to make her look at me this way? Could she be staring at my hair?

Mother was drying her face and hands on a flannel and speaking in quiet tones about the journey and the weather. I gave my face and hair a glance in the mirror, but did not wish to linger. I had never found a way of making my hair do as I wished and I would not find it now.

"Shall we go down?" I said.

As we returned down the staircase, a tall young man moved noiselessly out of the shadows at the end of the hall. I am well bred enough not to stare at a new acquaintance (even when they have just materialised from a tapestry), but the same could not be said for this gentleman. Under his dark gaze, I began to wonder if I had better go back upstairs and wash my face after all. Perhaps there was a particularly distracting coal smut on my nose.

Gwendolyn was saying something about him—Simon Drake, a neighbour on the most intimate terms with the family—and introducing me as 'Cousin Edith'. Good heavens! I hoped he would not consider himself licensed to address me so.

He took my hand and bowed over it in a singular manner. I could not make up my mind if he was trying out for the part of the tormented hero in a Gothic novel, or had simply copied his manners from someone much older and quite removed from modern life. Well, at least I need not expect familiarity from him, after all.

"Miss Worms," he said in a low voice, with a slight Yorkshire burr that was not unpleasant. "My condolences on the great loss to your family." His eyes were very dark, almost Latin, and matched the richness of his voice.

Let me be frank with you: I am generally suspicious of eligible men. My attachment to the single life is profound. I have found that the best course is to start off with new acquaintances by adopting a forbidding expression. It is a simple matter to put off young men in this way. One can always thaw a little later, once the risk has been properly assessed.

I drew myself up (I am short in stature yet I can command respect when I wish). "Mr Drake," I intoned glacially, moving aside for him to pay his respects to Mother.

Gwendolyn's eyes flickered between me and Drake. I congratulated myself on my coldness. There must be very few eligible young men of her class in this remote place and I had no desire to lure what must be the chief one of the district away from her. I wished I could inform my cousin that (despite my apparently shocking hair) I have had plenty of opportunities to marry if I chose. She had nothing to fear; her sweetheart was quite safe from me.

There followed an awkward repast, served in a very curious sitting room, with a low stone ceiling, intricately ribbed and vaulted, with traces of frescoes from long ago. But there was a fire here, and tea: both quite hot, thank God. This interlude was made bearable by my stepmother's indefatigable capacity for small talk. Shortly after, we endured a tedious meeting with the ancient family solicitor, which we were all obliged to attend, except for George, who had disappeared into the grounds in the company of a very large dog. Childhood does have its benefits.

Drake was there, his dark clothes, hair and eyes seeming to draw all the shadows in the room to him. His presence was evidence that he had some sort of unofficial but significant role in this family. Suitor to Gwendolyn or *de facto* male relative; or possibly both?

After a short but dreary summary of the legal situation and the extent of the property, things degraded quickly.

Father kept insisting that he didn't wish to disinherit his nieces. Ancient solicitor kept insisting that one couldn't play about with an entail.

"That's the whole point of an entail: one can't do as one likes with the property. My dear young man,"—this to my father, who was in his forties—"do you wish the great estates of England to be depleted as they have been in France? Even if you were to somehow recuse yourself, by what means I know not, the property would go to the next male heir, who happens to be your son. I fail to see how that might assist these young ladies at all."

I touched Father's arm gently.

"Father, let's not trouble this gentleman any further. He's quite right to insist everything be done properly." I lowered my voice. "Remember our plan." This was to remind him of my intention of writing to a London solicitor for help in breaking the entail and dispersing the property to our cousins, who otherwise would depend on our charity for their survival.

The dismal party then broke up, with Mother going upstairs to rest and Father going in search of a long-remembered library, accompanied by Drake who offered to show him the way. Violet and Una disappeared on some errand of their own.

That left me and Gwendolyn alone. I took matters into my own hands.

"Cousin Gwendolyn, I would very much like to walk in the grounds. I feel quite cramped from the long journey. My brother is somewhere out there with a dog. Perhaps I may meet him."

To my surprise, Gwendolyn insisted on accompanying me. Once we were outside on the gravel walk, she addressed me. "Do you mind—I wondered—you said to your father that you had a plan. What did you mean by it?"

"Our plan is to seek expert legal help on how this property might be more equitably disposed of, a plan my father is quite intent upon."

"Disposed of?"

"I suppose it seems foolish to you, but we have no desire to supplant you here." I now had a chance to make it quite clear that we were not here as usurpers.

"Why would it seem foolish?"

I felt slightly taken aback. What had I expected? Perhaps surprise, or gratitude; some acknowledgment that we weren't trying to take her home and lands from her. "Well, I suppose most people wouldn't be quite so eager to give up their inheritance as my father is."

This was met with silence. I decided to plunge ahead. "I don't suppose—would it distress you very much if the property was broken up and sold?"

At that she stopped walking entirely and stared at me. Her intense gaze was so puzzling to me that I regret to say I lost my head and began to retract my words.

"I mean to say—"

She cut me off. Her tone was utterly flat. "You couldn't sell Wormwood Abbey. You don't own it. The Abbey owns us. We serve this place, all of us, until we die."

I was so astonished I could make no reply. Gwendolyn began to walk again. "I will show you the cloister herb garden. It was laid out by the monks in the twelfth century."

CHAPTER TWO

I t was on the following day that I made progress on my other plan: securing a proper place to write. I had no intention of losing another whole day of my work to this house or its inhabitants.

Unlike Catherine Morland, I had fallen asleep immediately upon being shown my room and after the discomforts of the day I slept to a respectable morning hour.

My bedroom was entirely unsuitable for writing; the light from the antique mullioned windows was romantic but too dim by far. I was sure a house of this size must have somewhere I could make use of without ousting anyone.

Violet, being the most friendly and least gothic member of the family, was my choice of accomplice on this quest.

"Violet," I began when I'd finished my breakfast.

Indeed everyone but Violet had finished and left the two of us alone in the wood panelled dining room. Mother had gone out into the gardens with Gwendolyn and Una. George I had hardly seen. Father murmured something about the library and disappeared. Violet stayed at the table and ate steadily. I think her plan was to eat everything that had been left.

"I want to look for something. Can you help me find it?"

Her eyes got round and she stopped chewing. "What is it?"

"I want a study—somewhere quiet. Somewhere I can write."

She looked relieved. What had she thought I was looking for? "Library?" she offered.

"No, my father has taken the library. It won't do for me to write there, he'll talk to me. He'll read out bits of books to me every time I have a thought, and my thoughts will run screaming away."

She giggled, then thought for a moment.

"It has to be someplace that nobody wants and where nobody will talk to me. Somewhere a little bit secret."

Her eyes brightened and she jumped up, plunging her toast into her pinafore pocket. "Oooh, come with me!"

I had to hoof it to keep up with her. Violet was sturdy but fleet footed.

We went up and then down stairs and through several passages and ended up at a small door of obvious antiquity. Violet grinned up at me and gave the door a vigorous push.

I breathed a deep sigh of pleasure. The room was an octagon. We must be inside a tower, on the ground floor. The windows faced an aspect I had not yet seen. I could not have told you which aspect as I have absolutely no sense of direction. They looked out over expansive grazing land to the horizon, which was dim with mist. I felt pleasantly removed from the rest of the house and its doings here. I would bother no one. More importantly, no one would bother me.

"Do you like it?" She bounced on her toes.

"It will do very nicely. Thank you, Violet. I think you are my favourite cousin." I glanced at the empty fireplace. "Do you suppose…" I began.

"It's not far from the kitchen. I'll ask Pip."

She vanished, leaving the door slightly open. I could smell a faint aroma of cookery from the passage. We must be near to the kitchens.

I examined the room. It was sparsely furnished, but suited my purposes. It had a feeling of disuse, but was not musty or abandoned — it had been recently dusted. I noticed that the bell pull had been deliberately tied up so it hung out of reach. I had not noticed bell pulls in any other room. Well, I would not be pulling it anyway. I wanted to be left alone.

There was a serviceable desk, which I dusted with my handkerchief, and a few reasonably comfortable pieces of furniture, which being about fifty years old were the newest objects I had seen in the place thus far. A woven birdcage in one corner contributed an unexpectedly bohemian touch.

Violet darted in again, a bundle of sticks under her arm and a boy of about ten years of age in tow. Clearly a servant, the first I'd seen, he carried a pail with hot coals. It was a relief to know the Abbey was not staffed by invisible servants like those of the enchanted Beast in Madame de Villeneuve's story.

I was soon admirably set up. The first thing I did after getting my writing case from my bedroom and selecting a suitable chair was to write to my stepmother's cousin, Stephen Fairweather, who lived and worked in the City of London and had many friends in the legal profession (it was he who assisted me in finding a publisher for my work, faithfully preserving my anonymity as an author).

I enclosed a description of our situation and asking for a solicitor from a respected firm to be sent to the Abbey to research and advise on the possibility of breaking the entail. This task done, I settled in to continue the adventures of my dear police inspector.

I had done a good chunk of work when a figure passing by the window reminded me that I still possessed a human body that needed to be regularly tended and fed.

The human outside the window proved upon further inspection to be George, dripping and covered in duckweed. Clearly George had been having as satisfactory a morning as I.

Once in the passage, I followed the smell of food. I was soon in a huge kitchen of many flagstones and few conveniences. The cook, a middle-aged woman, looked up in surprise. I myself was equally surprised to see Gwendolyn in an apron, setting food on a tray. She stopped when she saw me. The three of us shared a moment of mutual discomfiture.

"Cousin Edith, I thought you were in your room," said Gwendolyn rather severely.

It suddenly occurred to me that Gwendolyn might not be pleased that I had commandeered a study without her knowledge.

"I was writing a letter," I said evasively, feeling like a schoolgirl.

Another servant, a strong, flaxen-haired young woman, came in a door rather in a hurry and stopped short, adding her surprise to ours.

Gwendolyn whipped off her apron and handed the tray to her.

"Lily, take this. I will show my cousin to the dining room."

I followed Gwendolyn through a series of passages,

some quite dark interior ones. She moved quickly and deci-
sively. I searched my mind for a way to put myself on a
better footing with her, but I felt oddly timid in her presence. I was no stranger to the kitchen at home, and did not
think less of Gwendolyn for finding her there, but
somehow catching her in that setting felt all wrong. I would
never have put one of my brave and beleaguered heroines
in a kitchen apron.

Presently I found myself in the Hall once more.

"Was this where the monks dined?" I asked.

"Yes, we eat in the dining room nowadays, but this was
the main refectory. There's an upper one too, it was made
into the library. Have you seen it yet?"

"Not yet."

"I'm surprised. Aunt Emily says you are quite the
scholar." This was said in a perfectly polite tone but
somehow I did not feel it was a compliment. Did she think
me a blue-stocking? I bridled a little.

"My father is the real scholar. He could have been a
professor, but he had a small daughter to raise and his own
way to make in the world, quite by himself, without the
help of his family. He was lucky to get a curacy at all,
though it hardly kept us from starving." I was getting
flushed now. "After he married my stepmother, well—she
had connections, or Father would never have got to be the
rector of St Giles. We are quite comfortable now."

I wondered if these words were too pointed. I wanted
her to know that we had won our comfort and happiness
without them, that we didn't need the Abbey and the
whole Landed Gentry could go hang as far as I was
concerned, but if she recognised the intent behind my
words she showed no sign of it.

We were now in the dining room and I was mildly
peeved to see Drake was present. I had felt more at ease at

breakfast in his absence. He felt like a shadow to me; a very tall, very masculine shadow.

As usual, my stepmother's gentle chatter eased things. "Oh, there you are, Edith. Were you lost? Gwendolyn has been telling me how labyrinthine the passages can be in this house. Perhaps she can give you a ball of yarn to find your way."

"I don't intend to hunt down any monsters, Mother," I joked. "The Minotaur is safe from me." I caught a glimpse of Gwendolyn's face and saw that it was quite blank. Whatever kind of education the daughters of her class received, it seemed it didn't include many Greek myths.

"Good," replied Mother. "Please don't, George brings me quite enough monsters as it is. Speaking of which he is putting on fresh clothes after his adventure. Don't let's wait for him."

"I glimpsed him from a window. Is there a pond, or did he make it all the way to the river?"

We all sat at the long table. Violet answered me, beaming. "I told him about the newts in the pond." She seemed proud of her success as a guide to the natural wonders of the place.

"Ah, I see you are on the way to becoming George's favourite cousin, also."

At this point Lily, the housemaid, entered with the tray to add to the food already on the sideboard and the meal began. I smiled at her, to no visible effect. I had seen three servants by this time, and they all seemed as strong and about as friendly as Vikings on a raid. Father had told me the Norse influence was strong in the Dales, and I believed him.

George soon joined us and gave a report on the newts, which had been highly pleasing ones.

Father had his head in the clouds, which wasn't

unusual if he'd found a book to interest him. He roused when I mentioned my letter, however, which Gwendolyn gave to Lily to put in the mailbag.

"Thank you, Edith. Now Gwendolyn, as I've been telling Drake, I'm quite in earnest about this. But before I proceed I should like to know what your wishes are."

Gwendolyn's eyes were cast downwards. She paused, then spoke slowly. "This estate has always passed to the eldest son, since the Abbey was gifted to us in 1537. It is what has kept the estate together. Without the entail, we would not exist."

"I understand that. But customs change, families change. I have no wish to play the part of Mr Collins in this one."

There was a sound, perhaps a muffled laugh, from Drake's end of the table. Surely he hadn't understood the joke? I glanced at him. He was watching my father with great interest.

"We claim to be a Christian land," continued my father in a softer tone. I recognised this tone as the one he always used when he was going to shock his respectable parishioners by suggesting they follow the tenets of Christianity. "And St James has told us that true religion is to comfort widows and orphans in their distress."

Her eyes snapped up at this. She took a deep breath and spoke quickly. "There is a cottage where my sisters and I could live, contentedly. There's no necessity of bringing in solicitors with all their fees to carve up the property. You might have the Abbey to yourself. We wouldn't bother you. You're not used to Ormdale. Our local ways will be strange to you. We might help you."

There was something extremely pathetic in this speech. It was the most unguarded I had yet seen her. I realised with a shock that the unguarded Gwendolyn was very young, and maybe even afraid. I felt ashamed of how I had tried to needle her over her family's behaviour only a little while before.

My father put his hand over hers. "My dear, we cannot remain here forever. I have a duty to my parishioners, and I must return to it. You yourself, having been brought up here, are by far the most suitable person in the family to oversee this estate, if you do not wish it to be sold."

Gwendolyn's lip trembled. "Excuse me," she said in a ragged voice, and pushing back her chair she left the room.

Mother looked as if she would go after her, but Drake rose and followed her out with a muttered excuse.

Mother and I exchanged a knowing glance. Perhaps this might be an opportunity for him to declare himself to her, if he hadn't already. I felt slightly comforted in the hope that Gwendolyn and her sisters might soon find a familiar and hopefully less chilly home for themselves on Drake's neighbouring estate. The proceeds from the sale of our estate (which father intended to share equitably) would surely sweeten the deal and expedite a marriage.

I decided to go for a walk after lunch, before returning to my new study. Experience has shown me again and again that a little air and light exercise is more conducive to a healthy literary output than shutting oneself up in a garret for hours on end. Many times a brisk walk of thirty minutes has solved what might have taken hours at a desk.

I turned my steps toward the ruined part of the Abbey. This was my first good look at it. It was obviously the remains of the Abbey Church. There was a circle of sky high on the end wall where a rose window must have once glowed with colours. The drain spouts were fashioned after some monstrous figures, but so worn away by the elements it was not possible to determine what kind.

I soon saw that it was possible to wander in through a

bit of crumbled wall, and drawn by a clump of primroses growing through a crack in the pavement I did so. I was bending to pick one to adorn my study when I became aware of two people walking past, outside the ruin, but quite close.

Now, I know it's a tired convention in novels to say 'they began to whisper intrigues before I could make my presence known' but I'll have you know it is a perfectly human reaction to go rather quiet when one overhears something like the following interchange.

"You'll just have to make her fall in love with you." This was said in a very matter-of-fact way by a young woman.

"You make it sound so easy, Gwen." I recognised the man's deep Yorkshire tones as belonging to Drake.

"Well, you made me fall in love with you," she retorted.

A low laugh from Drake. "And how precisely did I do that?"

Then they passed out of hearing.

I was now pretty keen not to be seen, so I waited for a while before emerging from my hiding place. I found my heart was beating a little quickly.

I could make no sense of what I'd heard. As the only single female of marriageable age currently on the scene, I felt certain they were speaking of me. But why on earth was Gwendolyn urging Drake towards me if she herself was in love with him? And what possible good would it do either of them to involve me in their affair? The scene was like something out of *Wuthering Heights*, a novel I heartily disliked.

As I made my way back to the study with my primroses I realised something else. Drake had laughed, as if Gwendolyn's admission of love meant nothing to him. And that laugh had been the same one I'd heard at the dinner table when Father made his joke about the entail in *Pride and Prejudice.*

Which meant that firstly, Drake was an absolute beast. And secondly, he knew his Austen. And that was a paradox I could not fathom.

CHAPTER THREE

I arrived back at my study to find the fire almost out. Taking up a sheaf of old papers I'd found in the desk, I fanned the coals back to life with them. The boy Pip had left a basket of logs and I selected the smallest of these to repair the fire.

Once it was lively and crackling I thumbed through the papers, which seemed to be some kind of old summary of housekeeping accounts.

"Laundry bills, perhaps?" I said to myself in amusement, remembering Catherine Morland's encounter with the same in another Abbey.

But that set me thinking of Jane Austen, which led me quickly to Drake's laugh and the strange interchange I had overheard.

This plot to ensnare my affections seemed both stupid and spiteful. Yet I had thought Gwendolyn neither of these. Just this morning I had glimpsed the unguarded young woman beneath the aristocratic veneer, and I had felt…curiously protective. Una was like a nerve laid bare with no defences against the world (I had little patience for that), and Violet seemed to have no nerves at all, but Gwendolyn—what was she?

My eyes fell on the primroses on my desk. That was what she was like, a green thing struggling to live between inhospitable slabs of stone. Fragile, beautiful, and determined.

I shook myself and set back to work, but was vastly irritated to discover that the afternoon's events were not at all congenial to my literary aspirations. Inspector Green was worthy of my best mental efforts and he was not getting them.

I put a larger log on the fire and kneeled on the hearth rug to gaze into the flames. I seemed to see a shape, as of a creature the colour of flame curled up among the coals. Any moment I knew the fancy would pass and I'd perceive some other shape. But it didn't. The creature was gazing at me with one eye, its long neck curving backwards over its body. The position was odd, but it reminded me of something I had seen before somewhere. It was then that I realised what I saw was no fancy but a living reptilian creature.

I was seized with a strong impulse to save the creature from burning. I jumped up and caught hold of a dagger-like letter opener on the desk. I quickly slid the flat of the blade under the creature's body and, with a panicked flick of my wrist exactly like turning a pancake, tumbled it out onto the hearth rug.

I sat on my heels. I half expected it to crumble into ashes. How long had it been there, in the fire? It did not move but slowly changed colour on the rug—it was now black with pronounced yellow bands on its belly and yellow specks elsewhere.

I felt a pain in my hand and realised I had been burned on the knuckle of my right thumb. I put it in my mouth

All of a sudden, the creature moved. Its neck straightened out from its goose-like position and its body swivelled right round. It faced me. It had tiny hands of five spatulated digits, splayed out. Its entire body was about the length of my own hand.

I blinked when its tongue flickered out towards me. Could it possibly be forked?

It ran at me with a queer alternating gait. I had no time to react; before you could say Jack Robinson (who ever does?) it had curled itself into my lap. It then went completely still except for its threadlike tongue, which whisked silently in and out.

It was most definitely forked.

This creature had claimed me as its own. I had inspired it to trust me and it now looked to me for protection and care. I looked down at it and wondered if this was how new mothers felt; this mixture of possessiveness, pride, and perplexity.

I reflected on my limited experience of domesticated animals and concluded the creature would need food, water, and a place to sleep. I hadn't the smallest idea what it ate, but I knew where to go looking for this information.

I remembered the bird cage in one corner of the room. I coaxed the creature into it, placed my own cup of water inside, fastened the door of the cage and went in search of the library.

THE LIBRARY WAS a long room over the great hall, divided up with many bookshelves. Father was poring over a number of open books on a table and scribbling in his notebook.

"Father, what is the name of that creature that Francois the First of France put on everything?"

"A salamander?"

"Yes! I remember now, the Salamander King. Where would I find something about them?"

"The Capets? Or salamanders?"

"Salamanders. I know quite enough about the Capets and I suspect that of the two, they are the lower life form."

"There's a natural history cabinet near the window seat." He went back to scribbling.

There was a generous window seat overlooking the cloisters. I was surprised to find Mother stretched out there, hands folded, in an attitude of idleness I found quite startling. At home she was always busy putting together baskets for the sick, writing to orphans, sitting on committees, teaching the destitute handiwork, and what else I hardly knew.

"Why, hello," I greeted her.

"Hello to you."

I came upon the cabinet of volumes Father spoke of.

"I've been thinking, Edith," Mother said thoughtfully as I scanned the bindings. "It's difficult to discuss things freely at meals. We should meet here each day. Just before tea?"

I took this in. "How long do you think we'll stay here?"

"I don't think we can leave until we've seen this solicitor you've sent for. And your father and I would like to leave things on a better footing than we found them. It seems to me that things are not quite as they should be."

I looked up sharply from a seventeenth-century Englishman's account of the flora and fauna of the island of Ceylon. What had Mother seen, or sensed?

"Whatever do you mean, Mother?"

"Well, the herb garden, for instance." She gestured towards the window, where the enclosed cloister garden could be viewed from above. "You can see the plan quite clearly. Your cousin tells me this garden dates back to the eleven hundreds. But I'm quite sure some of these plants are anachronistic. And the herbs were not cut back at the appropriate time. Don't you think it ought to be restored?"

Restoring a monastic herb garden to its medieval glory was so far from my plans that I did not answer. At present my most pressing task was to find immediate nourishment for a fire-resistant salamander. After that, I might turn my attention to the problem of my perplexing cousin and her intrigues with the neighbour.

The books were exclusively old and I found that my family's taste in naturalism ran rather to the fanciful. I took up Edward Topsell's *Historie of Four-Footed Beasts* and his *Historie of Serpents.* I was not sure if my salamander counted as a beast or a serpent, but it surely must be one of the two. Such books were sure to supply amusement if they failed to provide information.

"Are you writing, Edith?" mother asked, as I started to leave.

My heart warmed. My parents had always encouraged my work, even if they were not naturally disposed to appreciate my desire to contribute to the sensational literature of our nation. "Yes."

"Good," she said. "I think I'll rest for a while."

"I'm sure it will do you good, Mother."

My father made an exclamation. Then he called out a line or two in sonorous Anglo-Saxon.

"Isn't that ingenious, Emily?"

"Marvellous, dear," she replied, gazing out at the garden.

I left, grateful I would not be asked to admire Anglo-Saxon stanzas every few moments. Mother was a saint.

On the way back to my tower study I reflected that up

until this point in our history, our little family owed every bit of good fortune that had come its way to Mother.

Golden-haired Emily Fairweather had been the teacher at the village school where my father was a desperately poor curate with a small daughter, entirely alone in the world. Emily's family was liberal-minded enough to make no opposition when she chose to join her destiny to his.

I felt some satisfaction that their confidence in allowing her to make her own choice had been thoroughly justified in the happiness of our family. The unexpected developments which led us to the Abbey might raise our social position in the eyes of the world, but they could not increase our happiness.

I made a detour to the kitchen. The room was empty and there was an appealingly laden tea tray. A few burnt edges of gingerbread and some apple peelings had been discarded on the kitchen table. I put these in my handkerchief and made my escape.

I was afraid my salamander would have made his own escape by now, but I found him unconscious in his cage. I bent over and gazed at him. His scaled sides throbbed with life and he twitched occasionally as a dog does in its sleep. Possibly his ordeal by fire had exhausted him.

I checked my watch. It was tea time, which explained the laden tray. I slipped the fragments of food into the cage. The creature lifted its head and fixed me with one eye. Seemingly satisfied of my intentions, it transferred its attention to the food. The slender throat pulsed as it swallowed. Teeth were noticeable.

"I'm going to tea now, Francis. I'll bring you something more to eat later."

Francis. I had named the creature quite naturally, with hardly a thought. How odd, yet how normal it felt, to take charge of him. George was the one who was always bringing home animals and talking about them when one would have thought no one could have found anything more to say.

"I must ask Gwendolyn for the key to this room," I told myself as I went to tea.

When I arrived, Gwendolyn seemed to be making up for her uncharacteristic fragility at our previous meeting by acting the perfect hostess in the kind of way that sets everyone slightly on edge.

To my disgust, Drake was again present, listening intently to my father as he talked about the epic poetry he'd discovered in the library. I gritted my teeth when Drake's sleeve brushed against mine while reaching for his cup of tea. It was like having tea with the Abbey ghost.

George and Violet were as thick as thieves and getting crumbs everywhere. Una looked forlorn and saintly once again, even while eating gingerbread, which seemed a little unnatural. Mother spoke quietly to me, "Someone ought to pay attention to that child."

"Una? She seems quiet and well-mannered enough to me."

"Far too well-mannered. She's exactly like you were when I met your father."

"Me?" I recoiled. "How dreadful! Mother, why did you never tell me? No wonder I never had any playmates to speak of."

"One can't tell a child that sort of thing. Especially not a motherless one who has buried her heart in a box." Mother concluded this remark with a calm sip of her tea.

This unsettling conversation was interrupted by Gwendolyn moving to sit near us.

"As it seems you'll be with us for a little while longer, I wanted to have a word with you about the dangers of the environs."

Oh, really, I thought. *Is one of them this sepulchral fellow you want me to fall in love with?*

"Aunt Emily, I'm thinking particularly of your son." Gwendolyn went on to catalogue a spine-chilling list of perils, from falling masonry in the Abbey ruins to the fast-flowing river nearby. I felt that she was saving the worst until last. She paused for an instant.

"Finally, you are perhaps aware that this country is made up of limestone. You may not know that there is a vast network of caves, completely unexplored, the extent of which remains unknown."

All at once it seemed that everyone in the room was listening. Drake was fingering his pocket watch. It was the first sign of nerves I'd seen from him. What did it mean?

"Good heavens!" said Mother. "Have people been lost in them?"

"I'm afraid so."

At this, Drake spoke up. "Mrs Worms, when George wishes to trake about the countryside he is welcome to borrow my dog. He will be quite safe in his company. Pilot knows the country like none other, and would never let George go somewhere that would endanger him."

This was by far the longest speech I had heard from him and had the air of being rehearsed. But my mind latched onto one word: Pilot. A curious name for a dog with which I was nevertheless very familiar. But where had I heard it before?

Mother thanked him with relief for this offer.

"Is there treasure?" my brother asked unexpectedly.

Both Gwendolyn and Drake turned towards him.

"Is there hidden treasure in the caves?" he asked again.

Father beckoned to George. "There is no treasure in the caves. But there might be treasure here in the Abbey. I've found a number of volumes which I believe to be quite rare, George. And as for those newts, you might discover a new species, quite unknown to science." He put his hand on George's shoulder. "This is a wild countryside and anything might happen. *Here be dragons*." He had lowered his voice to just above a whisper at this last line. It was a saying Father and George had whenever they were in a ticklish situation, for instance when a particularly difficult parishioner was expected to tea and one's p's and q's must be minded.

Once again I sensed a breathless expectation in the room. Gwendolyn was looking at Father with an expression I found hard to define. Was it a mixture of hope and dread? But what was it that Gwendolyn feared, exactly? And for what did she hope?

CHAPTER FOUR

I t is an odd habit of mine that I often wake at moonrise when the moon is full. On that particular night, I had company during my moonlit waking.

I had brought Francis up in his cage after the rest of the family had gone to bed. I knew that reptiles were cold-blooded so I put the cage close to the embers of the banked fire when I went to sleep.

I woke to a bedroom lit with a milky light patterned by the mullioned glass of the window.

Then I realised that Francis was jumping about in his cage. Had the creature gone moon-mad? I got up and opened the cage and he ran up my arm and sat on my shoulder. It should have startled me but it didn't. He was now completely still, a calm presence, brushing not unpleasantly against the tendrils of hair near my ear.

Something made me go to the window and look out. I almost gasped at the ghostly beauty of the outlines of the ruin and the landscape outside.

I pushed the window open all the way to enjoy it better. The sky was crowded with stars, the moon swollen near the horizon. I had not realised how dingy with town-smoke the sky was at home. Francis made a slow clicking sound. It reminded me of a kitten's purr, but somehow scaly.

I think my salamander and I could have bathed in that light for an hour or more, had my reverie not been broken by the movement of a figure. It moved silently, darkly clad, along the garden path towards the ruined part of the Abbey, where it disappeared. It would have remained incognito, were it not for the presence of a large dog, which shadowed its steps, and was easily recognisable in the moonlight.

Pilot, Drake's dog. Francis stiffened on my shoulder, his little digits furrowing my nightgown.

All of a sudden, I knew exactly where I had heard the name before. Pilot was the dog of Rochester, that villainous and inscrutable man in Miss Bronte's novel who kept a secret prisoner in his dark ancestral abode.

I shut the window, shut up Francis, and got back into bed.

For the first time since arriving at the Abbey, I felt a chill of fear.

THE NEXT FEW days passed uneventfully. Drake was mercifully absent. I made progress on Inspector Green's latest case, which slightly mollified my impatience at being temporarily uprooted to a place which lacked the modern conveniences I had been used to at home. It was ironic to discover that our normal way of life as a humble clerical family was decidedly more comfortable than our cousins' was in the revered Landed Gentry.

A letter had come from a law firm in London promising the imminent arrival of a man named John

Rivers, who we hoped would make the crooked paths straight for us.

Father had had a letter from his curate saying all was well in the parish, and his Bishop likewise had encouraged him to be zealous in performing his family duties. Wormwood Abbey was far too remote for to'ing and fro'ing: much better to get everything settled at once.

Francis continued well, in omnivorous fashion. He was liveliest at twilight, and seemed content to be locked up in his cage when I went out as long as he also enjoyed times basking close—alarmingly close—to the fire on cold days. On warmer days he explored the room or perched on my shoulder and watched dispassionately while I wrote. I suppressed the impulse to ask him what he thought of the manuscript so far.

I had made no progress in discovering the kind of creature he was, though I found Topsell's seventeenth century bestiary an entertaining diversion from plotting a complex murder mystery that involved train timetables (I had brought a Bradshaw with me to consult, a lucky precaution as it turned out the Abbey library contained nothing so practical as this).

Topsell's advice on curing indigestion in dragons was amusing — like Aristotle, he asserted that it was caused by eating apples, and that lettuce would alleviate their symptoms. I wondered how many people in Shakespeare's day had need for dietary directions for sick dragons. While inwardly scoffing at myself, I abstained from giving Francis the apple peelings I spotted on the kitchen table.

I knew Francis was not a dragon, for the simple reason that dragons did not exist. I assumed that Topsell's "dragons" were actually exotic reptiles misclassified by credulous Europeans. Francis was clearly a misplaced creature of the tropics, that explained his lust for heat.

How he had come to this place I did not know. I still obeyed a nameless impulse to keep my scaled companion a secret, which rather impeded investigations into its provenance.

One afternoon, I was giving Francis a chicken bone on the rug in my study when a shadow crossed the window.

I felt sure before I looked that it would be Drake. He stood with his back to the window, gazing out across the fields, as if waiting for someone. Gwendolyn soon joined him and he presented her with a brown paper package.

For the first time since meeting Gwendolyn I saw an expression of unalloyed delight cross her face. I had always thought her an elegant woman but now I saw that she was beautiful. I found myself feeling more kindly towards Drake than I'd thought possible, simply because he had made Gwendolyn look like that.

She turned towards the house and her eyes fell on me through the window. Her face quickly hardened into its usual expression. By the way she turned on her heel and marched purposefully along the side of the house I guessed she was heading my way.

I scrambled to my feet. What was it about my cousin that so easily made me feel like a naughty child?

I turned to put Francis in his cage (I could easily conceal it behind an armchair) but to my dismay Francis had disappeared. Horrified, I hunted about for him wildly.

By the time she tapped on the door I had given up hope of hiding him. I could only hope he would keep himself out of sight while Gwendolyn was in the room.

"Come in," I called out with as much *sang-froid* as I could muster.

Gwendolyn opened the door and as usual I felt she took immediate command of the room.

"I see you've made yourself quite at home," she stated

in tones that were not exactly welcoming. I felt she was silently judging me for all the small alternations I had made. Was it very plebeian of me to have moved the sofa closer to the fire, I wondered?

"Violet was kind enough to offer me this room for my work," I blurted out, and then cursed myself doubly.

It was unfair of me to blame poor Violet who had kept my secret so scrupulously. And I'd had no intention of letting Gwendolyn know that I was a writer. As far as she knew I spent my hours indolently in my bedroom (when I wasn't making myself a nuisance by poking around the kitchen looking for scraps for the strange pet I had hidden from her).

Gwendolyn eyed the dusty volumes of Topsell, one of which was lying open on my desk, and her jaw became rather tight. Was she about to excoriate me for removing books from the library?

A slight movement caught my eye. Oh, there he was! Francis was creeping across the wall behind Gwendolyn. I spoke quickly so she would turn to look at me.

"Did you receive a package in the post?" I asked brightly.

To my surprise, she looked slightly abashed. "Yes. It's just a book."

"Just a book? I assure you I am quite alive to the pleasures of a new book." Good gracious, why was I speaking like this?

"Well, I'm quite sure you wouldn't approve of this one." (What was I, her maiden aunt?) "It's a detective story. It's full of murder and dark deeds and I know before it begins that everything will go terribly wrong and I won't be able to sleep at night until I finish it."

"I see," I said this because I did see. She might have been describing one of my own stories.

"Do you? I'm quite sure you'd find it terribly silly, compared to the books *you* read," she said with a note of bitterness in her voice.

I was about to protest when she unwrapped the paper and held up the yellow-covered volume defiantly. Oh dear heavens, it *was* one of my own stories.

"But I also know that the dear Inspector will untangle all the snarls, evil will be punished, good will be rewarded, and all will be right with the world. I dare say you find it facile. Perhaps it is. It's not like the real world at all—that's why I love it! Now I must be going. I've a household to run."

And with that she was gone. I sat down, with a mixture or relief and frustration. Goodness, what had set her off like that? And why did I find myself caring? I reflected upon it.

Francis scurried down the wall and across the floor to nestle in my lap. I looked down at him ruefully. As I'd said to Mother, I'd never had much of a genius for friendship. I'd never even cared much about a pet before this. The people closest to me were my parents and brother, and I was deeply grateful for them. Perhaps I've always been a little too conscious of my role as clergyman's daughter to make intimate friendships outside of my family circle.

My father's parishioners ran the usual human gamut from dear good souls to dreadful termagants but I'd not found one among them whose mind met my own in the way I demanded of an intimate friend.

And then there was the matter of my work. Another barrier to friendship was that I had chosen to preserve my anonymity as an author, out of reluctance to expose myself and my family to impertinent remarks. Model clergymen's daughters did not have an encyclopaedic knowledge of household poisons.

And how could one have true friendship without honesty? Perhaps, also, it was simply easier to let people conjure up their own version of me than to explain who I really was.

What a mood I was in. No, I must waste no more time worrying over Gwendolyn. She looked down on me, thought me a bourgeois snob. I flushed. Why should I even trouble to explain who I really was to her?

Then I remembered her words. "The dear inspector," she had said, and she had spoken of loving my stories. Here was praise indeed, without any possible insincerity. I smiled. Whatever was troubling her so deeply, over-work or nerves or unrequited love or the deaths of her relations or the fate of an inheritance, my books gave her joy.

I put Francis on my shoulder and returned to work with a zeal.

I worked late and missed tea, so I made my way towards the kitchen in hopes I might secure a bit of bread and cheese for myself.

I rubbed my eyes; they were tired from straining in the candlelight. At home we had gas laid on. How much easier everything was at home.

Cook had gone to bed. It was Gwendolyn I found, polishing silver at the kitchen table. The silver was arranged before her in careful lines and gleamed in the candlelight. The handles were wrought with an intricate design.

She looked up only briefly when I entered, but it was enough for me to see that the storm had passed.

"I'm sorry to trouble you. Like an idiot I missed tea." I quietly helped myself to what I wanted from the larder.

Then I stood watching her for a moment. She looked

like the Lady of Shalott, if that lady had been doomed to polish silver instead of weave by night and day. It was the second time I'd surprised her at household work. The first time she had seemed startled and displeased. This time she seemed merely resigned.

"I always imagined in these kinds of houses that the housekeeper did this sort of job." I paused. That was what had bothered me the first time. But now I was starting to understand. "But there's no housekeeper, is there?"

Gwendolyn continued methodically rubbing as she spoke in a low voice.

"There's no housekeeper. No butler, no footmen, no ladies' maids, no governess, no stable master, no groom, no head-gardener, no under gardener, no game keeper, and worst of all, no estate manager. My grandmother had all of those in her day. My great grandmother was presented at court. She had a capuchin monkey and went about the estate in a curricle and a bonnet with a feather in it. The monkey sat on her bonnet and played with the feather, I'm told. Can you imagine?"

"A monkey? In Yorkshire?" Despite myself, I sat down at the table with her and propped my chin in my hands to listen.

"Yes. Her husband was in the East India Company. He collected a menagerie of exotic creatures. They were kept in a sort of hothouse. I can show you where it was."

I perked up my ears at this. Why, this must be how Francis came to be here!

"It's all ruined now, of course," she concluded flatly. "There's nothing left now but a few bits of glass." There was that resignation in her voice again, as if the destiny of everything in her world was ruin.

"I'm sorry," I said after a moment. I picked up a spare

cloth and began on the knives. Upon closer inspection, the design seemed to be one of interlacing serpents.

We were quiet for a while. I didn't dare to speak. There was a companionableness to this moment that felt fragile, and I didn't want to be the one to break it. Then Gwendolyn looked at me.

"I didn't realise before you came that Aunt Emily was your stepmother."

My throat went a little dry. "Yes. My real mother died when I was a small child. Father was disowned for marrying her, you know."

"I didn't. I always thought he'd just…escaped."

"Oh," I was taken aback. All this time I thought Gwendolyn was looking down her nose at us: the black sheep, the outcasts, because of her family's rejection of my father. Had I been quite mistaken? I found I wanted to test this a bit further. "My mother wasn't from the same class, you see," I ventured.

At this Gwendolyn burst out laughing. I must have looked hurt for she apologised immediately.

"Forgive me! It's just…do you know what my father said to us every day of our lives? *We're not like other people.* You know the saying: they're in a class of their own? Well, it's true of us. There isn't anyone else in our class. It wouldn't have mattered if your father had married a Saxe-Coburg-Gotha or a washerwoman. If she was from outside the Dale, then she was nobody."

I digested this for a moment. In this moment, I thought, this one fragile moment that I suddenly wanted to hold in the gentlest of hands, it seemed suddenly possible for us to be friends. And I was about to risk it all. But I had to know whether a friendship between us was really possible or not.

My mouth was so dry now I regretted the bread and

cheese I'd eaten. I longed for a cup of water but I couldn't get up now, it would be like running away. It was now or never.

"She was a Jew," I said simply.

At this Gwendolyn stopped polishing and looked at me across the table. "Oh," she breathed.

I kept my eyes on the knife I was polishing. "She had to leave everything, her people cut her off completely when she converted. I believe she'd been quite well off. It must had been hard for both of them, having nothing at all but each other."

"So you and your father…really had no one?" Gwendolyn's voice was soft. Was it possible that she wasn't drawing back from me?

"Yes, exactly. Until Emily came along. Dear Mother, she's been everything to us."

"Do you remember her? I'm sorry, I've no right to ask."

"No, please! I wish I could remember her better. Just a warmth that was there and then it wasn't. That's all. And yours?"

Were we really sitting here talking about our dead mothers, just as if we were ordinary cousins and as if our upbringings had not been worlds apart?

"Ten years ago. The '89 Influenza, just after Una was born. It took my grandparents as well, and some of the Drakes, and many of the older Dale folk." Gwendolyn went back to her polishing.

"You've lost so many people," I realised. Was that why she was afraid?

"I suppose I should say 'not as many as some', but yes —I've lost so many people."

"I'm sorry I never met them."

"Don't be. They didn't have time for anyone outside the estate."

"And the Drakes?"

"Ah, the Drakes are almost family. You know they are a sort of cousins of ours? I mean, not close ones," she hastened.

Of course she'd say that; she wants me to marry one, I thought. Now was as good a time as any to disabuse her of this notion.

"I'm not sure I quite like Mr Drake, he's a little too Heathcliff for me," I said as lightly as possible.

"But Simon's marvellous," she exclaimed, her eyes wide.

"Each to his own, or her own." I shrugged and smiled. By this I meant to let her know that I had no designs on her lover. She might be ready to hand him to me on a silver platter but I was handing him right back.

"By the by, he was here the other night. I saw him out my bedroom window. Does he always take his constitutional in the dead of night in other people's gardens by the light of the full moon?"

I could have kicked myself. Gwendolyn's shutters instantly went up.

"I asked him to stay that night. One of the shepherds was complaining of a wolf taking lambs, not far from here. It unnerved me. I'm used to having my father and brother about the place."

Somehow, I knew without a doubt that she was lying. *Oh, Gwendolyn.* I felt the precious moment of candour between us dissolve.

"We should go to bed." She packed the silver away neatly in a box, locking it with the help of a ring of keys from her pocket. So many locks and keys.

"That reminds me, might I have the key to the study? I

should hate one of the children to mess about with my papers." I kept my voice normal. I didn't know much about making friends, but I supposed anything of the sort would take time, and couldn't be grabbed at.

She looked at me, holding the keys. "Of course," she said at last, unhooking one of them. "That was my mother's room."

"Oh! I'm sorry…"

"Not at all." She handed it to me briskly. "I saw your light under the door, as I used to see hers when she was doing the accounts. It felt companionable, knowing you were there."

I felt a flutter of hope as I took the key. Companionable. That's how we had been together, a moment before. And she had not rejected me because of my mother. Perhaps we might find our way to such a moment again.

"Enjoy your book," I dared to say as I slipped out of the room. Did I see a faint smile on her face as I shut the door?

CHAPTER FIVE

Rivers arrived two days later. He was a younger man than I'd expected, light-haired and well dressed. He had already met with the aged solicitor and was well acquainted with the conditions of the entail. He smiled a great deal more than anyone I'd met so far in Yorkshire, and I noted this with an odd jolt of recognition. Here was a man of my own class, the professional class, who reeked of town living: hackneys and gaslight and functional plumbing and empty smiles at the people who paid the bills. Was this how I appeared to the people here? Or had I become gothic myself in so short a time?

"As I understand it, sir," he addressed my father, "as well as advising you on the entail, you'd like me to give you a thorough summary of the financial situation of the estate."

"Yes," I interjected. "The financial situation seems to us to be quite dire, and our family is very anxious that my cousins be provided for. There seems to have been no annuity for them, or indeed any provision made for their maintenance whatsoever."

While I spoke he waited with an air of patience, then turned back to my father. "I understand you are anxious to provide for your nieces and you have concerns also as to the financial viability of the estate at present."

I stared at him. What was wrong with the man? Hadn't I just said that exact thing myself?

Father spoke pleasantly but firmly. "Mr. Rivers, my daughter is my confidante in all my financial matters. It was she who wrote to your firm. We act as one in this affair."

Rivers said, "Of course," and bowed his head slightly to me, as if he was ready to treat me as a rational human being now that my Father had given him permission to do so.

Inwardly fuming, I went to find Gwendolyn and ask her for the estate books. I found her in the midst of one of her regular *tete-a-tetes* with Drake.

"Why does he want them?" she demanded.

"Because we want to see you and your sisters provided for, of course, and we want to know if the estate can do that." I may have snapped at her a little, due to my present mood.

Gwendolyn turned towards Drake, as if looking to him to provide a way of escape.

Drake touched her arm, warning her with his eyes.

"Of course. I would be happy to help Mr Rivers go through the books. There will be some irregularities, and he may need a guide."

Gwendolyn nodded, and seemed relieved.

Good heavens, these men! How many of them wanted to turn women into clinging ivy to their stone walls? Well, Drake's was one wall I was not going to cling to under any circumstances.

I stomped off to the study and did a good couple of

hours of work on a knot of alibis and train timetables. "Well, Mr Rivers, what do you think of that!" I pronounced to nobody in particular.

Now that I could lock my study I allowed Francis the run of the room even when I left it. It was always interesting to see where he had got himself to when I returned to it. His favourite spots were the hearth rug, the sunny window sill, and hanging from the disused bell pull. He had already grown in size by wriggling out of an intact skin (this gave me quite a start; I used my handkerchief to put it in a drawer) and was now bigger than my hand. It was dawning on me that I might not be able to keep him in this room forever.

On this particular day I closed Francis in his cage when I went up to tea. He had made rather a mess of one of my pages of notes and I did not want a repeat of *that* performance.

I went up to tea feeling slightly sour. I hoped Rivers would take his tea with the estate books and not with us.

But Rivers was with the family when I arrived and I soon saw that he had lost no time in irritating Gwendolyn also. Her aristocratic disdain was a sight to behold.

Apparently the man was an amateur naturalist in his spare time and had discovered that the Abbey had once housed a menagerie.

"How sad nothing was preserved, Mr Drake. Not even a skeleton? Or an egg? I understand any specimens have not been looked after but I would not be averse to adding some items to my own collection, if their condition is not too bad."

Gwendolyn's lip curled as she poured out.

George stopped gobbling tea-cakes for a moment. "I've found some newts, Mr Rivers, and some rather unusual feathers. Can I show you?"

Rivers laughed. I disliked his laugh immediately. "I'm afraid there aren't any amphibians living in Yorkshire that could interest me, my boy. Anything you could find in the dale would be quite in the common way."

George looked disappointed.

"Are you quite sure about that?" I broke in.

Everyone turned to look at me in surprise.

"Because I've a creature in my study that I'm sure is quite out of the common way."

Rivers's asinine smile wavered. "What kind of creature?"

"Unfortunately the reference books here at the Abbey are not adequate to identify it. I thought at first it was an amphibian, but I now think it must be a reptile."

It was then that I noticed something odd. Gwendolyn made a sudden movement and her cup of tea sloshed on her lap. It must have been very hot because she had just poured it out a moment earlier, yet she made no sound at all. An instinct stopped me from drawing attention to it by offering her my handkerchief.

Rivers looked at me with real interest for the first time. "How intriguing. I should be most glad to identify it for you, Miss Worms."

I felt instantly that I'd made a stupid mistake. I had been so precious about Francis I hadn't breathed a word about him to my nearest and dearest relations. Then this horrid man came along and by his rudeness provoked me to reveal him to all and sundry.

As the conversation moved to other subjects I glanced at Gwendolyn. She was utterly pale, almost deathly so against her black dress. Yes, I must have done something stupid indeed.

As I rose to leave, Gwendolyn intercepted me near the

door. Rivers had been about to follow me but Drake drew
him aside to speak to him.

"I need that key back." She held out her hand to me.
Was it trembling?

"But—"

"For God's sake, I'll explain later. Please."

"But what am I to do with—"

Her tone was low and urgent. "For the sake of any
friendship that has ever been or ever will be between us."

It was the first time she had spoken to me of friendship.
My heart jolted. I placed the key in her hand immediately.
She took a breath.

"Thank you. Take the long way."

Rivers caught up to me.

"Miss Worms, will you be so kind as to show me the
way?"

"Of course."

Gwendolyn said she must have a word with the cook
and would join us shortly.

I do not like to dwell on this part of the story. Leading
Rivers in a circuitous route about the Abbey to give Gwendolyn time to do I-don't-know-what was not my finest hour.
While in truth I have a terrible sense of direction, I am
usually quite capable of finding my own room in a house,
and pretending I could not rather hurt my pride. When we at
long last we approached my study I had no way of knowing
if I had taken long enough for whatever Gwendolyn planned
to do. I was now throughly flustered and it was easier than I
liked to admit to play the part of feather-brained female.

"Oh, here it is! At least I think…oh, what a bother, it
appears to be locked. Now, I wonder…"

Gwendolyn stepped out of a nearby doorway with
slightly flushed cheeks. Drake was with her.

"Cousin Edith! Your key. I found it."

I took it with a slight glare. "Goodness, however did I drop it?"

The three of them followed me into the room. Francis's cage was where I left it, covered with a cloth. I often left it this way. I could not remember if I had done so on this occasion.

In the midst of many uncertainties, I felt quite certain that whatever confronted us upon the removal of the cloth would not redound to my credit. Rivers extracted an eyeglass from his pocket. I saw he had a notebook with him also.

I could delay no longer. I gritted my teeth and pulled off the cloth.

It was a horrible moment. We all stood and stared at the small, pale, damp creature in the cage. Finally, Mr. Rivers cleared his throat. "I believe, Miss Worms, that this—"

Gwendolyn and Simon spoke at the same time.

"Isn't it a sort of newt?"

"A newt, I think?"

My voice, when it came, was bitter. "Yes. I must say, this afternoon it seems *regrettably newt-like*."

Drake's eyes flickered over to me and I thought I saw his mouth compress.

"Well, as I said," Rivers chuckled, putting away his glass. "There are no uncommon reptiles in the Yorkshire Dales. Of course, not being a herpetologist you could not be expected to know that, Miss Worms."

I had no wish to prolong this humiliating charade. "If you'll excuse me, I believe we both have work to do."

Gwendolyn ushered Rivers out, throwing me a look of gratitude. Drake lingered for a moment but I pointedly seated myself at my desk with my back to him and this soon saw him off.

In spite of my coldness I was of course madly curious as to why this charade had been enacted. I was also oddly relieved. I had instantly regretted revealing Francis's existence to Rivers. But I was also angry at Rivers for his superiority and at my cousin and Drake for subjecting me to it.

Most pressing of all, where was my salamander? I felt a rising outrage that he had been removed from my care, and a deep concern for his wellbeing. I had never felt so protective about anything in my life. It was a curious feeling, sparking within me both pleasure and pain.

I wasn't going to get any work done in this frame of mind. I confronted Gwendolyn and Drake in the kitchen, where they seemed to have collapsed in relief at the table.

"Where is Francis?" I demanded without further ado. Drake stood up.

Gwendolyn raised an eyebrow. "Who is Francis?"

"It's what, not who. Where is he? I won't have him detained in some cold and gloomy chamber. And I should like an explanation." I sat myself down at the table and crossed my arms. Drake sat down again.

Gwendolyn took a deep breath.

"Of course. You see, your Francis is rather a...rare kind of creature."

"So I suspected."

"And Rivers...he might make things unpleasant for us all. Bring all sorts of amateur naturalists down upon us, if you see what I mean. And then close upon their heels come...the tourists." She shuddered, as if she could hardly bring herself to say these words.

Drake now seemed more than usually somber. What on earth had I done to offend him? It was I that was offended against! I took a breath and reminded myself of Gwendolyn's hardships before I spoke.

"Dear cousin Gwendolyn, I have come to understand your family likes to shroud itself in mystery. I'll do my best to not stir up a hornet's nest of undesirables in the form of daytrippers and naturalists, but please, would you be quite frank with me in future and not manage me like some sort of querulous aunt?"

Gwen's lips twitched with amusement (I don't know what was funny). "I will try."

"Mr Drake," I said rather sharply. "I'd like Francis returned to my study at your earliest convenience."

Drake went very still, if that were possible for someone who habitually vanished into the panelling. His voice was more than usually low when it came.

"Miss Worms, are you aware the creature is dangerous?"

I stared at him. He went on.

"Are you aware that the creature moults periodically? And that ingesting even one minuscule fragment of its skin would mean instant death?"

"Mr Drake! I am not in the habit of ingesting the skins of my domestic animals, even in minuscule fragments."

"Nonetheless—"

At any other time I would have had the presence of mind to question him about the creature. What else did Drake know about him? But I had had enough of supercilious men for the day. "I remind you of my request," I almost snapped. "And of my promise not to pursue the subject further with Mr Rivers."

"Thank you, Edith," Gwendolyn said quietly. It was the first time she'd called me by my Christian name without attaching 'Cousin' to it and I found I liked it. She had also spoken to me of friendship. She lifted her eyes to mine and they were very solemn.

"And now *I* have a request. You said I should be frank with you and not manage you. I ask of you the same. If you find anything that disturbs you in this house, or on this estate, I beg you to tell me at once."

I nodded, slightly quelled. I felt I had made two mistakes: keeping Francis a secret from Gwendolyn and revealing him to Rivers. These were minor infractions, surely, but they felt heavy and I did not understand why.

I rose to go about my business. Drake stood and stopped me with a small motion.

"Miss Worms, if I may trouble you…why Francis? The name?"

Why on earth would he care what I named it?

"Because of the Salamander King, of course."

Now, what on earth was this expression on his face? Was he pleased? He bowed slightly.

"Please, don't let me detain you further. I will return Francis to your study at once."

With an unpleasant sensation of having passed an examination, I went back to my work.

CHAPTER SIX

After this episode I avoided Rivers as much as possible and counted on Mother to give me any legal updates during our daily meetings. Francis had been returned to me, seeming none the worse for his ordeal. Mother said that Gwendolyn was increasingly cross-grained about anything to do with the finances or the future of the Abbey. After my conversation with her that night in the kitchen, my belief was that Gwendolyn, having been raised in such seclusion, was quite unable to imagine a life beyond the one she had lived, though living it seemed to bring her little joy.

During the incident of the substituted salamander I felt that we two had made a little progress towards friendship. We had reached an agreement to treat each other with more honesty than heretofore. I'd been affected by her appreciation of my novels and I found myself longing to hear more of her opinion of them. One evening we met by chance in the hallway en route to our respective bedrooms. I seized my chance.

"How did you fare with your novel?"

To my dismay, Gwendolyn's face clouded. "I didn't finish it."

I'd always wondered what the Psalmist meant when he said "my bowels have turned to water" and now I knew: he meant someone whose opinion he greatly cared for had told him one of his psalms was rubbish.

Gwendolyn gave a sigh. "It's silly of me, but…I'm afraid the inspector is being taken in by—by a woman who is very much beneath him. I can't bear to read further. You see, I admire him so much."

"Oh!" I blushed. She talked about my inspector as if he was a flesh and blood acquaintance and for some reason this made me feel terribly self-conscious. "But…these sorts of stories do that, don't they? Work you up to a fever pitch of nerves and then everything turns out all right in the end?"

She blinked in surprise. "What do you know of these sorts of stories?"

I cleared my throat. "I may seem like a blue-stocking to you but I am not too stuck up to enjoy a good novel I assure you." I hoped that didn't sound as if I'd rehearsed it, because I had.

"Oh. But that work you are always so eager to get back to…isn't it something very learned?"

"Well, I wouldn't say learned exactly." I didn't feel equal to confessing my authorship yet. One thing at a time. "But I've had an idea."

"Yes?"

"How would it be if I read ahead for you? I could tell you if it all ends badly for your inspector."

Her face brightened a little. "Oh! How kind of you. Are you sure? I'll bring it to your room."

I was brushing my hair when Gwendolyn came in. Brushing my hair always makes it stand out a bit around my head, like an absurd halo. I felt rather foolish as she presented the book to me.

"Thank you, Edith," she said. And then stared at me, the way she had the first day we met. "Your hair…"

"Yes?" What on earth was she going to say about my hair?

"It's in the family you know."

I almost dropped the hairbrush on my toe.

"What? In this family?"

"Yes."

"But who—"

"It skips a few generations and then it pops up again. It's quite a prized family trait."

I was stunned. "I always thought it came from my mother's family."

Gwendolyn had delivered the book but she now made no move to leave.

"Your mother must have been very brave, to do what she did," she said in a strained voice. "To leave everything she'd ever known. To lose everything."

My eyes pricked with sudden tears. I had not expected any sympathy for my mother in this house.

Gwendolyn sat on the bed and folded her hands in her lap, like a child about to make a confession.

"I know I haven't been terribly forthcoming. I was raised to be…reticent. My family had no time for outsiders. The estate was everything to them. If you have any questions, about the Abbey or our family, I'll do my best to answer."

I had so many questions. They flashed through my mind: why do you want me to fall in love with Drake when you care about him yourself? Why must you stay here? Why are you afraid? May I be your friend?

The question I blurted out was unexpected, even to me.

"How did you father and brother die?"

Gwendolyn's eyes darkened. My stomach tightened with dread. Had I once again chosen the wrong question?

"It was a hunting accident."

"Yes, that's what the letter said. But I don't understand. I've seen no hunting paraphernalia. Is there a local meet?"

"Oh," she said, her hands tightening in her lap. "No. Not that sort of hunting."

I waited. She swallowed.

"Last year we had a great deal of trouble with wild beasts stealing lambs from our tenant farms. Father and Percy began tracking them after the first thaw."

"I remember you mentioned a wolf," I recalled. She continued without acknowledging this comment.

"They tracked them to some caves. It was reckless of them. But the estate has been losing so much. We rely on our farmers, and they rely on us."

I would have stopped her, I wished to cause her no more distress, but she went on.

"Pilot found them deep inside the caves. A team of our people reclaimed their bodies. What was left of them. Simon would not let me see them. I gather they were much defaced."

I could think of nothing to say in response to such a horrible story. I tried to recall Mother's words when something awful happened. Suddenly I remembered her words to a woman in our parish, the widow of a drunken man who had destroyed himself.

I put my hand over hers. They were trembling. "You have suffered so much."

"And I will suffer more…unless your father takes over

this estate." She raised her eyes to mine. They shocked me by their bleakness.

"Gwendolyn! You can't mean to suggest we should all go on living here, after what you've just told me?"

She clenched her jaw stubbornly. "They shouldn't have gone after them. It would have been alright if they hadn't." This struck me as rather heartless.

I tried again. "My father has a vocation, he has a duty to his parishioners."

Gwendolyn removed her hands from mine and got up.

"He is a Worms. That means his duty is here."

"Gwendolyn!"

She spoke over her shoulder, in the coldest tone I had heard from her yet.

"You think you can escape it. But you can't. Not even you, Cousin Edith."

And she left.

THE NEXT DAY I found it quite impossible to get any work done. My thoughts were in disarray. I caught up Francis in his cage and took him with me to the old monks' garden inside the cloisters.

It was a pleasant day. The herb garden was a peaceful haven, open to the sky, in the middle of the dark stone passageways of the cloisters. There was a stone pediment in the middle of the garden which looked as if it should have a stone saint upon it. Today, I found Mother there with Una. The child was hovering by her elbow, looking up at her with great blue eyes every time she spoke, as if Mother *was* the saint. I had called her one often enough myself.

"Now, Una, I want you to choose one of these bulbs to draw. No, I won't tell you which one. You shall choose for yourself. Do you know the name of this fragrant one? Yes, you're quite right. And do you remember the story of Echo and Narcissus? No? Well, in a moment we shall sit in the sun and I will tell it to you."

There was a shout of interest from the cloisters and I looked up to see Violet and George running towards me. I let them inspect Francis through the cane bars.

"Do be careful, children," I warned. "I'm not sure, but I suspect he may bite."

"Do his bites kill people?" asked Violet, as if this was a perfectly normal question.

I was about to tell her not to be absurd, but her question brought to mind the gory demise of her father and brother and I thought better of it.

"Would he like a mouse, Eddie?" asked George helpfully. "I've got a mouse in my pocket."

"Of course you do. And he may indeed like a mouse. But I'm quite sure I should not like to see him eat one."

"Would he swallow it whole? Like the snakes in the Amazon?"

"Goodness, I don't think so. I rather hope not."

When they had tired of inspecting Francis I turned back to the house. I passed Mother and Una on a stone seat.

"So you see he was doomed to be quite alone always, gazing at his reflection. Though I never felt being transformed into a fragrant flower was much of a punishment. Now Una, would you like to look at Edith's rather unusual reptile before she puts it away?"

I paused for an instant to oblige, but Una shrank back against Mother with a look of unutterable horror.

"No? Never mind, dear. All of God's creatures are beautiful and useful in their own way but some of them are not very pleasant. Go on, Edith, I'll see you in a moment, just before tea."

From this pointed comment I gathered that there was something to discuss more significant than Father's current mania for Anglo-Saxon poetry. I nodded in acknowledgement then continued on my way. The weather was mild so I decided I would walk right round the house to the scullery door and make my way in there.

On a whim, I unfastened the door of the cage. I was fairly certain Francis was sufficiently attached to me not to disappear and I wanted to try him with a little more freedom.

As I came round the wall and into the yard where things were delivered to the kitchen, I turned back to enjoy the prospect of the spring sunlight on the hills.

I promised myself I would go for a long walk on the next day. On a long walk I could let my mind wander over and around the knot of alibis I needed to untangle, and perhaps I would happen upon the loose end I needed.

A dog barked. I felt Francis skitter about in his cage. Then Pilot shot past the yard and disappeared round the corner of the house. I didn't pay much attention to this, because just at this moment something rather more startling occurred to occupy my attention.

Francis clambered out of his cage and directly into my face. I made an undignified sound. The tip of Francis's tail slithered into my mouth and scudded across my teeth as he scrambled into my hair. He instantly settled his body snugly around my chignon and went still. I was vividly reminded of the story of the lady who wore the monkey on her bonnet, but an intensely bitter taste in my mouth put that out of my head.

Suddenly, Drake's warning about ingesting salamander

fragments resulting in sudden death seemed more significant than I had previously admitted.

It is strange to recount now, but I never doubted that the salamander scales were poisonous. As a child I had once nibbled on a leaf of foxglove before Mother seized it and threw it away, and this tasted far worse. Nor did it occur to me to spit the taste out of my mouth, which one should most assuredly do when one has been so foolish as to put something poisonous in one's mouth.

Though I have never believed in ghosts, I found myself wondering if I would haunt the Abbey grounds in exactly this form: a girl with a salamander in her shock of red hair. Perhaps George's children would tell stories about me such as I'd heard about the ancestress with the capuchin.

George. I felt a warm gush of relief that I was on good terms with him, as well as Father and Mother. This was followed by a pang of regret for leaving my dear inspector in the midst of an unsolved mystery, but it couldn't be helped.

I sent up a wordless prayer of repentance for my stupidity and pride.

Then I consigned my soul to God.

CHAPTER SEVEN

A few minutes later, I'm told, I stumbled into the kitchen where I demanded buttered tea-cakes from Cook and then burst into tears. I remember this only hazily. I was taken to my bedroom and tucked into bed by Mother.

She had come to look for me herself, with some notion that I would forget our meeting. She found me sobbing into my arms at the kitchen table like a ruined scullery maid.

Francis was coaxed from his unorthodox perch and back into the cage, then placed by my bed. Mother would not allow me to explain anything. She told me quite sternly that I'd been working too hard and she wanted to hear nothing from me until I'd rested.

I fell into a deep sleep. As happens when one falls asleep too early, I awoke at the wrong time. It was dark, but the light from stars and half-moon were bright enough to reveal a tray by my bed. And a mouse, nibbling at the food on it. Suddenly there was a scrabble across the floor and the mouse disappeared entirely into Francis. I covered my eyes with my hands. I felt quite sure that if I saw a wiggling mouse-shape in his small belly I would scream and wake the whole household.

I had disgraced myself enough for one day, so I waited until I felt sure the mouse must have expired for lack of air. Then I sat up. I glanced at the cage and saw that several of the wicker bars had been snapped. I was very sure of two things: the cage was not sufficient to hold Francis anymore, and I would sleep no more that night.

It was then that I heard the footsteps. I told myself that it might be another sleepless member of the household. I would peep out my door and see if it was someone with whom I might suitably share a few sleepless hours (Mother would be ideal), which would be a welcome relief from my spinning thoughts. But I felt the same chill of fear that had touched me the night I'd seen Drake prowling about in the moonlight. Suddenly it seemed of great importance to me that I get up and look out of my door. I refused to allow my brush with death-by-reptile to leave me weak and indecisive.

I softly crossed the floor, cracked open my bedroom door, and peered into the passage. At first I could see nothing. Then the darkness coalesced around a tall, masculine figure with his back to me, moving down the passage. Good heavens, what was Drake doing now? The figure paused in the faint checkerboard light of the mullioned bay window at the end of the passage. The figure was undoubtedly young, tall, and well-made like Drake, but the hair was light.

Rivers! What could he want, creeping around the house at midnight? Could there be an innocent explanation? At that moment he turned to look behind him. I kept utterly still. Then he went on his way.

I snatched up my dressing gown and belted it on over

my nightdress. Being a dark colour, it would help me to remain unseen. I crept out the door, barefoot, shutting Francis in my room to digest his mouse in peace.

I moved quickly but silently down the passage. That one furtive look behind him had been enough to convince me that whatever Rivers's business alone in the house at night, it was no trivial errand for bodily necessities. I disliked the man but I had not thought him dishonest. I felt a sense of responsibility for this man's presence at the Abbey. It was I, after all, who had written to summon him here. I wanted to know if he was up to villainy.

Once out of the passage I slowed down. I had no way of knowing exactly where he had gone, but he must have gone down the grand staircase in the Great Hall if he was going anywhere. I was considering which way to look for him when I reached the head of the stairs. A small light below me in the spacious Hall made me stop.

Rivers. He had kindled a light - which he had not done when it might be seen beneath a bedroom door - another proof of nefarious intentions - and was hovering near the tapestries on the wall. As I watched, he began to tentatively twitch at them. The first thing that sprang to mind was that he must be looking for a secret door behind the tapestries. I almost snorted. A priest-hole or a false wall for concealing valuables was not out of the question in a house of this age, but he was an idiot to be looking for such a thing in a wall of solid medieval masonry.

My humour vanished. He had made a small sound of triumph. A sort of self-satisfied purr entirely in character with what I knew of him so far. Now he swept the tapestry up and aside with his arm and gazed at something. I could see nothing of it as his arm was towards me and the lamp was screened by the tapestry he was holding aside. I gripped the banister. What on earth had he found in the wall?

He carefully rearranged the tapestry in its original position, then swung round and moved swiftly towards the stairs.

Up until this moment I had been so gripped by curiosity I had not considered any danger towards myself. But now it occurred to me that I did not want to confront this man alone in the dark. I could not run. At the speed necessary to outrun him to my bedroom I could not be as noiseless as I had been when I was following him. The thought of being chased through the passage in the dark was intolerable.

He was now ascending the stairs at a smart pace. The small circle of lamplight was not yet near me, but I had missed my opportunity to escape.

Some memory of a successful game of Hide and Seek with my brother inspired me. In an instant I folded myself into a huddle on the landing where I hoped the shadows were deepest. I hid my face in my arms—it might show pale in the lamplight and draw his attention. Hiding my face thus, I could not observe him when he drew near me. I was fortunate, I thought, that my dressing gown and hair were of a similar hue to the carpet on which I crouched. I hope in his haste and the dim light he would simply pass me by.

But he did not pass me by.

I heard and felt the dull thud of his steps stop as he drew opposite me. I did not breathe at all. It was horrible to imagine him staring down at me when I could not see him. What would he say? What would he do?

I was just gathering my nerves to jump up and scream for help when he moved on. I waited for a few moments, then dared to draw a ragged breath and unfold myself.

Had he seen me? But if he had, why leave me there without confrontation?

I got up and peered around the door into the passage, just in time to see his door shut gently behind him in the starlight. Of course. He had stopped before going into the passage to extinguish his lamp, a task which must have distracted him enough to overlook me, huddled on the carpet at his very feet. I leaned against the doorframe and breathed a few times in relief. When I was calmer, I went into the passage myself.

I hesitated by Gwendolyn's door. Ought I to rouse her now and tell her what I'd seen? I thought of Gwendolyn's exhaustion, evident in her tight face. Rivers had surely concluded his investigations for the night. It would be better to tell her in the morning, when we were both in full possession of our wits.

I took myself back to my room. Francis was in a soporific state, no doubt induced by the current exertions of his digestive system.

I sat up for a while to ponder this odd episode. If I was inventing this scene for one of my inspector's cases, I would have laid clues leading up to it. There would have been talk of some kind of mystery, perhaps a hidden legacy. The solicitor would have perhaps believed himself to be the true heir to the estate, looking for evidence of a secret marriage. But this was fanciful and I could think of nothing that would make Rivers's actions comprehensible.

One thing I determined upon. First thing tomorrow, I would find out for myself what Rivers had seen under that tapestry.

THE DAY DID NOT PROCEED as I had planned. I purposefully arrived in the Great Hall at the breakfast hour, so the other members of the household would be occupied while I attempted to recreate Rivers's discovery. I had just stretched out my hand towards the tapestry when there came a clanking sound behind me. I gave a strangled yell and whirled around.

There was the servant Lily, lugging a large metal pail and a heavy mop.

"Oh, dear! You gave me quite a start, Lily."

She began to mop the floor. I walked back and forth, pretending to be greatly interested in the tapestries. They turned out to portray harts, eagles, and dogs in a herb garden. I did not know how long I could go on pretending to care about them. Lily dutifully mopped. I was dismayed by the very small patch of floor that had occupied her attention for the last five minutes.

"Is this your day for cleaning the hall, Lily?"

She gave me a look that said I had clearly lost my mind and must be treated carefully. "Yes, Miss."

She moved into a ray of light from the high clerestory window. It burnished her fair hair so that I had to blink. Perhaps Lily was more than a housemaid. Perhaps she guarded this Hall, like a Danish shield-maiden of old. I brushed away the absurd thought.

"These tapestries seem a little dusty. Will you take them out and beat them today?"

This stopped her in her tracks.

"No, Miss. They were cleaned last month. They only get beaten once every spring, Miss."

She went back to her task, which was clearly going to take all morning. I gave up and went to breakfast. Shield-maiden or housemaid, Lily was not leaving the Great Hall anytime soon.

Gwendolyn was absent, as was George. Father was looking very serious, as if he had an unpleasant job to do.

Mother was looking excessively sweet, as if *she* had an unpleasant job to do.

Rivers, on the contrary, was in high spirits. I found his neat appearance—well brushed, well pressed, well built—exceedingly unpleasant this morning after observing his nocturnal hijinks.

"Sir, I must compliment you on your nieces' elocution."

Violet and Una looked up from their breakfast.

"Indeed? Must you?" asked my father. "You may certainly compliment them, but I have had nothing to do with my nieces' elocution."

"They speak very well. You need not be ashamed to take them into society with you."

Mother glanced at the girls in discomfort.

"I shall never be ashamed to take them anywhere, no matter how they speak, if they are kind and honest, as I hope they are," Father replied. I could see he was deeply irritated. Rivers, apparently, could not.

"Yes, but take your neighbour, Drake—excellent man, I'm sure—but speaks like a sheep-herder. Your father made sure to send his sons off to the right schools to make men of them. Drake told me he was educated at home. No way to build an Empire, eh?"

Rivers accompanied this last comment with a smile and a forkful of eggs. My fork had stopped halfway to my mouth. I looked at Father.

Mother turned to Violet and Una. "Girls, I believe I left our sketching things upstairs in my room. Run and get them for me and we will go do our Nature Study in the garden."

Father waited until the girls left the room, and then spoke very calmly. "Mr. Rivers, my own time at 'the right school' was such an unmitigated torment to me that I only wish my father had had as much care for me as Mr.

Drake's did for him. As for the Empire, if we must have one, I'd vastly prefer it to be watched over by sheep-herders than tyrannised by men whose souls have been brutalised by the kind of 'education' (as you call it) that I was forced to endure. You may recall, perhaps, that Our Lord was not ashamed to call himself the Good Shepherd, even if you do not seek to follow His humble example."

I thought for certain this would have buried him but I had underestimated Rivers.

"You misunderstand me! I heartily approve of Christianity," he said this with a smile, as if my father would be delighted to hear it.

Father's eyebrows shot up.

"It has provided this country with an admirable ethical code, which belies its humble origins as the cult of a primitive Eastern tribe. Combined with the elegance of Greek philosophy and the incomparable discoveries of Modern Science, it has done very well for us, and I believe we may partly credit our present success to it."

Good heavens, I thought. Not content sneaking about our house at night like a burglar, he had to go lecturing my father on Christendom over breakfast. Mother picked up the teapot. "Another cup of tea?"

Father pushed his cup of tea aside. His tone was now curt in the extreme.

"Mr. Rivers. I must thank you for your assistance in this matter of the entail. You know your business, I think, and I am grateful for enlightening me on many legal details which were opaque to me."

Rivers's face froze. Mother shot me a pregnant glance, as if to say, *Now you see what we wanted to discuss with you yesterday.*

Father pushed back this chair. "My wife and I will decide how we wish to proceed and contact you by post."

"Sir, have I offended you in some way?"

"Have you offended?" my father repeated. "Have you offended? Why, yes, if it comes to that, you have, sir. You have made impertinent remarks about my nieces. You have treated my daughter with contempt. You have insulted our neighbour and intimate friend, a gentleman who gave his time to assist you. And you have spoken irreverently to me, a clergyman. I thank you for the services you have performed for us and ask you to remove yourself at your earliest convenience."

"Sir, I beg—"

Father rose to his full height and spoke in a stentorian tone that I'd never heard him use from the lectern. "That will be all."

Rivers left the room.

I picked up my tea cup with a contented sigh. "What a beautiful start to the morning, Father. Being the Squire Apparent of Wormwood Abbey suits you. I think you should use that exact tone on Mrs Withers next time she gives you trouble about the bell ringers."

Mother laughed. Father sat down.

"I think I may have overdone it."

"Not one bit. And I'll tell you why," I began.

At that moment George burst into the room.

"Sorry I'm late, Mother! Is there any food left? I was following a dragonfly. It was simply enormous! What a ripping day."

I had just been about to tell Father that Rivers's impudence ran deeper than he had guessed, but I hesitated to do so with George in the room. I didn't like the thought of George knocking on the walls night and day looking for secret passages and driving Gwendolyn out of her wits.

"Edith, what were you going to say?" asked Mother.

George sat himself down to diligently consume eggs.

Father reached out to ruffle his hair. It was fair and glossy, like Mother's. George began to describe the dragonfly to father in detail. How alike the two of them were in their passion to understand the world around them. Father had his archaic languages and George had his creatures, but it was the same somehow. What did I have? A talent for imaginary crimes?

"I'll tell you later. I'm going to go find Gwendolyn. Do you know where she is? By the by, did she know we were giving Rivers the boot?" I asked Mother this quietly, so as not to disturb George's natural history lecture.

"Yes, I spoke with her yesterday. She was most relieved. Apparently the man had been making himself troublesome to the whole household."

More than you know, I thought. I got up to leave, looking out the window at the sunny day appreciatively.

"I thought I might go for a wander on the hills today."

"Fells," said George, who had finished about the dragonfly and thus overheard my last sentence.

"What?"

"They call them fells, not hills," he said matter of factly, between bites. "And you 'trake' instead of wandering."

"Oh, well, then, a trake on the fells. How romantic it sounds."

"Don't get lost, dear, romantically or otherwise," Mother said amiably.

I went in search of Gwendolyn. I wanted to tell her as soon as possible about Rivers. I noticed Lily was still hard at work on the floor in the Great Hall.

"Lily, do you know where your mistress is?"

"Miss Gwendolyn is going over the menus with Cook, Miss. She don't like nowt to disturb her."

I thought for moment. It was, as George had said, 'a

ripping day' and I felt high in spirits and longed for a ramble.

"I'm going for a trake on the fells, Lily. Tell my cousin I've something important to tell her and I'll see her before tea. Oh, and don't do my room today, Francis has chewed his way through his cage and is at liberty in there." I was going to have to find a better way to contain him, as I was now convinced that he was dangerous, if only unintentionally so.

I provisioned myself with a hat, a thick jersey, some stout shoes, and bread and cheese wrapped in waxed paper. Francis appeared to be sleeping off the mouse and hardly noticed me. I left a note for Mother saying not to expect me for dinner. All the time my heart was singing that I was alive and the world was lovely. I couldn't wait to be out of doors.

CHAPTER EIGHT

I set out towards the view seen from my study window: rolling pastureland and vast sky, which today was a rare and glorious blue. Every so often I came across a wooden stile to help me over the stone walls, and once I came across a flock of sheep with trembly new lambs. Lapwings guarded their unseen nests in the grass, and a vole darted along a wall.

What a fool I had been for not coming out here sooner. Had I been afraid to fall in love with this place? How silly of me; I could enjoy the beauties of this place without fear. We would find a solution to the problems of the estate and go home to our normal, workaday lives in good time.

In the meantime, what harm was there in revelling in the beauty of this peaceful upland after days inside, cudgelling my brains for the benefit of the reading public?

I could make out a rock outcropping in the distance; a pale slash of limestone in the green fells. It was not obvious how big it was, nor how far from the Abbey. I determined to go as far as that rock, and if I could climb it, sit awhile there admiring the view.

A thin, melodious singing came from above me. A lark. I squinted my eyes against the sunlight but I could not see it, only hear it, so high was it hovering. I felt quite of the same spirit as that lark.

After about an hour, I was close enough to the rock formation to see that it was truly enormous. The grassy incline I was on rose steeply, sloping upward to the top of the rock, and if I followed my present course I would find myself at the top of it in about another hour or so.

It felt a little hot in the sun as I climbed the hill, but I climbed it more easily than I had expected. Presently the ground levelled out and became curiously formed. I was walking on a kind of limestone pavement, like giant cobbles, with large cracks in between, from which peeked out ferns and wildflowers. I hopped from one to another like a child. I must bring George here, I thought. I must come to the cliff edge soon.

Looking up from the pavement, I stopped to gaze back in wonder at the way I had come. The vista was uninterrupted to the horizon. On the right, I could see the exposed and windswept Abbey, with its ancient ruined bell tower and the Renaissance-styled tower where I worked. It was all open land around the Abbey, limned only with ancient rock walls and gorse bushes blooming gold against the tender new green.

Arriving at the edge, I found it fell absolutely sheer to the river bed. I could spy a bird's nest on a ledge in the cliff below me. There was no water up here, so I surmised that the river must flow underground through the caves Gwendolyn had mentioned. If I was still, I could hear water far below.

The valley beneath me was full of trees. I could see smoke rising from somewhere among them. Perhaps a farm, or a shepherd's cottage. I knew there were tenant farmers, though I had met none of them.

This hidden wood below me was strangely inviting. I could almost believe in the stories of Faerie here. Who could say what kind of creatures might still play and hunt and feast in such a wood?

I sat on one of the largest rocks and ate my bread and cheese, listening to the cry of a curlew. I let my mind go quiet for a moment, and then I asked it a question. *Why?*

I thought I knew the answer. I felt so strong happy today because I was alive. I knew—somehow, I absolutely knew—that Drake had been right. Francis's scales should have harmed me. Why hadn't they? Had I been the recipient of a miracle?

Mother would say that every day is a miracle. That it is we who have grown so dull and stupid that we do not see it, expecting the miracles to go on and on, without recognising them for what they are.

I had grown dull and stupid; but today I felt like scales had fallen from my eyes. I'd been so selfish about coming here. Willing to do my duty—only insofar as it did not inconvenience me. Judging my cousins for their birth and circumstances, and how different their lives had been to mine, without considering what difficulties and disadvantages those very differences might bring.

The Abbey was now laid out before me as the folk of this country must have seen it for eight hundred years. It looked to me as if it was watching over the valley and the fells, as the shepherds watched over their flocks.

Whatever happened to this place, it ought to be taken care of. Was it to understand this that I had been spared?

For the first time, something about the place stirred my heart. It was a similar pang to the feeling I had for Francis.

It was a feeling of being trusted with something unexpectedly.

I got up and walked a little way across the giant paving stones. A tremendous longing filled me to descend into that valley. To return the way I had come would be simple; I could see the way from here, every yard of it. But I wanted very much to see the wood. Surely I could walk across the great rock and see if there was a way down into the valley and the wood. Once there, it couldn't be too hard to find a ford or a footbridge to cross the river. Perhaps I could call in at the place with the fire, and there would be a farmer or cottager there to direct me to the crossing and make my way back.

Mother's genial warning about getting lost wasn't entirely a joke. My rambles always turn out best when there is someone to tell me when I'm going the wrong way. But I felt confident to chance a different route home because I could see everything laid out before me like a map. Who could get lost in such a place?

I got up, wiped my hands on my handkerchief and set off across the great rock. After a time the ground began to fall away. I pushed through some scrubby bushes and saw that beyond them was a small ravine. I could see a way down into it, but I could also see that I must take care as the rocks here were very small; a kind of shingly stuff that was frighteningly easy to slip on. It took me some time to descend to the bottom of the ravine. And I still hadn't reached the wood. Well, I certainly wasn't going back *up* the ravine, so the only way onward was forward.

I followed the winding, leafless ravine, hoping it would lead me to the beautiful valley I had seen from the top of the Great Rock. This was a shockingly desolate place. It recalled an illustration in a copy of *The Pilgrim's Progress* I'd had as a child; a prize for memorising scripture verses. I'd been strangely embarrassed to win it. Of course I knew scripture verses. I was the Rector's daughter. I'd wanted no prize. I wanted to give it to the boy who had got second place, but Father told me that it was an exercise in humility for me to accept.

The picture had shown Christian and one of the horrible creatures that assailed him, crouching behind a rock, ready to spring. I tried to admire this savage land-scape but if I was honest, I did not like it at all, and I felt suddenly very alone.

I thought of the wolf pack that had recently killed my uncle and cousin. Would it attack by daylight?

I was close to losing heart when I turned a bend and saw green leaves. Trees, with delicate spring leaves, lime-green. I had found it! I was in the hidden wood. It was even more beautiful than I had imagined. It was Spenser's wood, Malory's wood, Shakespeare's Forest of Arden. I had felt a shiver of this when first entering the Dale by carriage two weeks ago. Now I was drenched in it. I wished I was a poet and not a detective novelist. The place was not savage as the ravine had been. It had a delicate Faerie wildness that agreed with my nature exactly.

I soon found the river and followed its course. I think I lost all consciousness of time for a while. I was following some kind of sheep path, which lulled me into a feeling of security. I was jolted out of my reverie when I realised that the river had widened due to receiving another tributary. I had surely missed my best chance to cross it. I realised I had no idea where I was. I might have already passed where the Abbey stood, high above, on the other side of the river.

"Romantically lost," I murmured Mother's words to myself. Suddenly I felt very tired. I looked behind me and was shocked by how far away the Great Rock looked now. I felt a growing sense of dismay.

What was wrong with me? Why did I feel like a little lost child? I decided to cheer myself up by singing the Doxology at the top of my lungs. You simply can't cry and sing loudly at the same time, and if you try, you'll only end up by laughing and then half of your problem is solved. I turned around back upriver and tried not to think of climbing up that slippery ravine alone, with a monster behind a rock watching me.

I heard a dog bark and there was a vigorous rustling through the tangle of meadowsweet, loosestrife, and wild violet. My hopes rose. Pilot burst through. I knelt down and rubbed his ears gratefully. His jowls flopped about companionably. Drake had said the dog was a reliable guide to the countryside; perhaps he would lead me to the Abbey. The dog turned and bounded back along the sheep path. I followed eagerly.

He veered off the path through a bush. I pushed my way after him. He took me slightly further away from the river. Now I could see smoke from a chimney and glimpse buildings through the trees. I stopped for a moment to collect my wits. Whatever household lay behind these trees was certainly not a cottage. Could it be…

From the corner of my eye I saw a dark figure. Drake. He was standing on the opposite side of a little stream. There was a quiet watchfulness about him. I'd often seen it at the Abbey and disliked being its object, but here in the woods it felt quite different. It was as if I was being watched by a character from a fairy story. A woodsman, or a prince of Faerie, perhaps. Watched, measured. As if he was waiting for me to do something, unable to speak until I did. To break an enchantment. But what enchantment?

In the end, he spoke first. "We heard you, singing."

"I was lost," I said simply. As if it was the most natural thing in the world to sing when one is lost in the woods. He nodded, as if it seemed so to him.

"You are trying to get back to the Abbey. My home is very close. Would it suit you to rest there for a while?"

I looked in the direction he indicated. I found myself oddly drawn to see those buildings behind the trees, as if something important waited for me there. Or perhaps it was just the prospect of a soft chair and hot tea that drew me.

"No," I said firmly. "I'd like to be back before anyone worries about me."

"There is an easier way. Would you allow me to show it you?" He asked this very courteously, as if it wouldn't be madness for me to decline. How different the man was from Rivers. Sheep-herder? What nonsense!

I nodded. He crossed the small stream nimbly and helped me across. I remembered how I had shuddered once when our sleeves touched, but his light, respectful grip did not trouble me now.

I saw with a jolt of surprise that he was missing the top joint of his left thumb, though whether this was an injury or a birth defect I could not determine.

We were now between the stream and the river, walking back towards the Great Rock.

"It is not far now," he said, to my relief. "You have had a long walk."

"Yes."

Soon he said, "Here is the crossing."

I exclaimed in delight. Someone had fixed perfectly square stepping stones to the riverbed after some mysterious fashion, making a delightful footbridge that did not impede the flowing of the waters. I was pleased that though he went behind me, he did not offer to help me here. I hopped from one to another as gleefully as a child.

When we had crossed, I found there was a wider path on this side of the river. As we left the river behind us and began to ascend an upward path I found that his arm was ready to steady me any time I might want it.

Now that we had left the wood behind us, it felt like a time for more ordinary conversation.

"You come this way very often," I observed.

"Yes. Our families have been close for several hundred years."

"Several *hundred?*" Well, perhaps not so ordinary, after all.

"Of course you know the Abbey was given to your family by King Henry upon the Dissolution."

I nodded.

"But perhaps you don't know that your family's connection with this valley predated that event by a very long time."

"Indeed?"

"I believe the last Abbot was one of your family."

"How surprising! And he made the change, along with the Abbey?"

"Yes."

"That is singular."

"It is. But there have always been Worms here. No one remembers a time when the Dale was without them. Perhaps he cared more for that than his religion. Or perhaps he honestly embraced the new faith. It's impossible to know."

"And your family?"

"Their history here began with Henry's daughter. We are newcomers compared to you."

I looked at him out of the corner of my eye, but he had said this with genuine humility.

"And why did Good Queen Bess take an interest? Don't tell me you're connected to Francis Drake the pirate," I laughed.

"We prefer the term privateer."

I glanced up at him to see if he was serious. As always, he was.

"Yes, I suppose you would. Are you a direct descendant?"

"The ancestor who built Drake Hall was Sir Francis's nephew. They were a very large family. Sir Francis was one of twelve sons. My ancestor was given his land in recognition of services rendered to Elizabeth."

"What kind of services?"

"The details are opaque."

"Was he a spy?"

"Perhaps."

We were silent for a little while. This was as good a chance as any to as a question I'd been curious about.

"Gwendolyn says we are related?"

"Yes. We share a pair of great-great grandparents. Perhaps, you would like to see their portraits. They are in the gallery at Drake Hall."

I found something off-putting about sharing ancestors with Drake. I remembered the plot to match us with distaste, for a different reason than heretofore. I changed the subject.

"Tell me about Pilot."

"What do you wish to know?"

"Was he bred on the estate? I wondered if perhaps an ancestor of his might have been known to my father during his childhood."

He thought about this for a moment. "Why?"

"It's nothing really. My father didn't have many stories of his childhood. He had them beaten out of him at school. But one he loved to tell us was about a summer evening when he…well, it's childish and fanciful, but he thought he saw a dragon in the garden. He described it as the size of a large dog. So naturally when I saw Pilot, I thought it might have been an ancestor of his that he saw."

The silence stretched out as we climbed. I wondered if I'd made a fool of myself.

"Why do you think it was a dog?" he asked after a moment.

"It seems the most likely explanation, doesn't it?"

He stopped. "Have you never thought, Miss Worms, that it might have been a dragon?"

I stared at him. Was he making fun of me?

"Well, Mr. Drake, I don't suppose I have." What else was there to say?

"Perhaps you ought."

We walked in silence for a time.

"I wonder if you have any idea how Francis came to be here?" he asked.

"Well, Gwendolyn mentioned an ancestor who once kept a menagerie of exotic animals. I thought perhaps Francis's antecedents might have escaped and naturalised in the woods nearby. As best I can tell, he seemed to come out of a log of wood I put in the fireplace."

Drake seemed to think about this for a moment. "And what kind of creature do you think him to be?"

"Well, I'm not much of a naturalist, I'm afraid. I think you must know much more about him than I do."

He was silent and I realised that he wanted me to give my opinion first. How different from Rivers! I continued speculatively. "At first I thought him some kind of amphibian, but his scales place him in the lizard family, I believe.

He certainly looks exactly like the things that Francois Capet called salamanders, which don't look at all like the kind of salamanders my brother has in his book of animals."

"Yes, the old kind of salamanders were creatures that were reborn in fire." He looked at me with something like a spark in his eyes. "And what is that, Miss Worms, but a dragon?"

The truth of it hit me at once. "Oh! Of course! That must be what my father saw in the garden, a creature like Francis. Why didn't I think of it before!" Another thought struck me, less pleasantly. "But…oh dear, is Francis going to grow as big as a dog?"

Drake looked away. Did I sense disappointment? Or relief? What was it? I thought I must have imagined it as the next minute Drake spoke quite normally.

"If he does come from the menagerie, there's a book you might use to identify him. It was written by a man named Knox who was held captive on the island of Ceylon during the reign of James. It's in the Abbey library."

I beheld in my mind's eye an old volume I had picked up for a moment while speaking with Mother in the library.

"Thank you so much, Mr. Drake. You have been most helpful."

I now felt quite friendly to the man. I did not wish to have him as a suitor but I could allow I'd misjudged him. We had climbed completely out of the valley and could see the Abbey, about half a mile from us.

"Are you coming to tea, Mr. Drake?"

"No, I'm expected home."

I wondered who would be expecting him, in the heart of that hidden wood. No one had mentioned any other Drakes.

"Well, thank you very much, Mr. Drake. I'm very glad you found me."

I offered him my hand to shake. He took it and seemed about to perform his courtly little bow as previously, but changed his mind and gripped it in the handshake I had intended. His grip was pleasant.

"It is nothing, Miss Worms." He turned.

"Wait. Pilot—"

"You'd like him to go with you?"

"No, no, I just wondered—the name?"

He raised his eyebrows slightly. Then he answered in his usual slow, thoughtful tones.

"Pilot has found a safe harbour for me many a time, just as he did for you today."

Of course, how simple. I felt the need to tell him why I had overlooked this obvious explanation.

"Oh, I thought…that you might be thinking of Miss Brontë's novel."

For a moment his look was a complete cypher to me.

"Oh. No. I don't like gothic novels." Then for the first time in my memory he smiled a full, slow smile. "I much prefer Jane Austen."

It was a smile of such a boyish sweetness, it took me quite by surprise. I'd never have imagined a face like his could produce such a smile. Then he disappeared down the hillside and I turned back to the Abbey. I found I had a smile on my own face.

CHAPTER NINE

To everyone's relief, Rivers had the good sense not to show his face at tea-time. I had still to tell Gwendolyn about my midnight excursion, but I would wait until we were alone.

Meanwhile, I made an effort to be especially attentive to the children. I'd devoted very little time to getting to know my younger cousins, so I asked them about their favourite books, thinking this would be sure to draw them out. I was dismayed to find them unable to answer the question at all. At their age, I had devoured Scott and Stevenson, but they seemed entirely uninitiated in these or indeed any fictional delights. I kicked George under the table to stop him from exclaiming at their ignorance and made a silent promise to send away for some exciting literature forthwith. Lang's Blue Fairy Book and *Treasure Island*, I thought, would make a good beginning.

When everyone was leaving the sitting room after tea, I stayed behind with Gwendolyn. She was tidying up the tea things and putting them on a tray.

"Lily said you wanted to speak with me?"

"Yes, it's about Rivers."

"Dreadful man. He's leaving in the morning, thank heavens."

"Yes, you should have heard Father send him packing. He was simply marvellous. He looked exactly like my idea of a squire. But that's not what I wanted to tell you."

"Is it about the book? Was it very dreadful?" Her voice was light but she seemed nervous. What on earth was she talking about?

"Oh!" What an idiot I was. I had promised to find out what happened at the end of her novel for her. Well, that didn't present much of a problem, since I had written it myself. "No, not dreadful. It was very entertaining in fact, in its way," I said this in a lofty sort of tone, and then I hated myself for it.

"But the inspector?"

"The inspector. Yes. I liked him." I suddenly remembered what had worried her. "He behaved with perfect discretion and good judgment, as always," I reported with great satisfaction.

She sat down with a sigh. "You have relieved my mind," she said.

Goodness, was it possible that she took these characters I had invented out of my head so seriously? Was that natural? All the same I loved her for it.

"I'll go get the book at once, only I really must tell you about Rivers, it's frightfully important, Gwendolyn." I absolutely could not allow myself to be distracted from this one moment more.

"What has the man been doing now? Stealing the silver?" she asked with a little twist of her lips.

"Yes! I mean, possibly. Is the silver something special? Did it belong to Francis Drake or anything?"

"Edith, what *are* you talking about?"

"I found him creeping about the Abbey last night with some kind of ill intent, I'm sure. Rivers, that is. Not the ghost of Sir Francis Drake."

"Creeping about the Abbey, Edith? Whatever do you mean?" Her face was blank.

"I followed him. He was pawing at the tapestries. I thought perhaps he was looking for a secret door and at first I thought him an utter fool but then it seemed as if he'd found something, only I don't have the least idea what it might be and I hoped you could tell me."

The blank look had vanished and now she had gone pale. I determined to have it out with her. My walk on the fells and in the wood had given me a dose of courage to speak to her more plainly than I had yet dared.

"Gwendolyn, I don't know what secrets you feel your-self duty-bound to guard, but I want to be your friend. Can't you tell me?"

"You've no idea how costly my friendship might be, Edith."

Costly? She was afraid, so afraid, of sharing her burdens with me. I felt a strange premonition that she was right, that pledging my friendship to her would come at a cost. I also knew with a deep and steadfast certainty that I wanted to do it anyway. But how to convince her? Being a true clergyman's daughter, I turned to Holy Scripture for the right words.

"We are to bear each other's burdens. I don't know exactly what burden it is you bear, Gwendolyn, but I'm willing to at least try to lighten it for you. *Two are better than one.*" I sat next to her and put my hand on hers again. This time she didn't take it away, but grasped mine tightly in return. She seemed so affected she could hardly speak.

"Tomorrow, after Rivers is gone, I'll ask Simon to

come. We'll tell you everything." Her voice cracked. "You should go."

I could see she didn't want to cry in front of me. I pressed her hand and then rose. "I'll put the book in your bedroom."

I went to my room with a light heart. I felt with Lady Julian that all manner of things should be well. Rivers was leaving, Drake was not the shadowy character I had thought him, and Gwendolyn was taking me into her confidence.

As I shut the door behind me I saw there was a fire in my bedroom fireplace. I stopped. It was a fine day and I had told Lily not to come in my room. Who had made the fire? And why? What if Francis had got out?

I saw to my relief that Francis was on top of the wardrobe. He was completely still, as if he was pretending he wasn't there.

"Francis! What are you doing up there?"

A man's voice behind me said pleasantly, "Please don't scream, Miss Worms."

I spun round. Rivers was sitting in a chair in the corner of my bedroom. I screamed.

"Well, there, you know, I told you not to scream," he said in a pained voice. "Because there's no one at all in this wing of the house to hear you. You'll only agitate the *varanus salvator*."

"The what?" I asked stupidly.

He indicated Francis.

"How trying of your cousin to make a fool of you the other day. You're quite right, you know. Those creatures are not usually found in Yorkshire."

I had gathered my wits about me again by now. I straightened to my full height. "And solicitors are not usually found in my bedroom, Mr. Rivers, so I'll ask you to leave at once."

"No maidenly hysterics, if you please, Miss Worms. My interest is in the varanid only."

This incensed me. "And what was your interest last night when you were sneaking about the house?" I snapped. Oh, no. What had I said? I quickly put my hand on the doorknob. He was far enough away from me that I could slip out before he could stop me.

"Oh." He blinked rapidly. "I see I was wrong to underestimate you. I really should have known."

"Should have known?" Blast the man, he kept saying things that piqued my curiosity.

"That you'd be sharper than the rest. The Jewess's daughter. It is sad to see a great English house in such decay. Inbreeding has been the downfall of many a noble family in this country. New stock is needed. It's the common hybrid that has the most vigour."

I was speechless for a moment at the man's rudeness, and felt strangely shamed at this reference to my mother. It all made me more angry.

"Please cease these vile horticultural metaphors. I demand to know what you came to the Abbey to find!"

He blinked again.

"You don't know. They haven't told you."

I was silent. I refused to be baited again.

He took out his handkerchief and began to polish his eye glass. "You must have seen things here. Things that aren't….what they seem. Things that don't add up. Your uncle and cousin, for instance. Did anyone see them after they died?"

What on earth was he talking about now? "Mr. Drake identified them."

"Ah. Drake. Precisely." He replaced the glass in his pocket.

"What exactly do you suspect him of?"

"The question is, what do you suspect him of?"

Oh, no, I wasn't going to be tricked into answering his questions. "Mr. Rivers, if you are quite done—"

"Not quite. I want to show you something. You'll want to see it, believe me. Now, you stand near the door. You can even open it a little if you want. Then you'll be quite sure I won't make an attempt on your virtue, won't you?"

I very nearly threw the wash basin at him for that. But I did stand near the door. I wasn't going to be tricked into doing the opposite of what he said just because he was so loathsome. He got up slowly and moved to the other side of the room, keeping his distance from me. Then he stepped onto a chair. He quickly reached up to the top of the clothes press and seized Francis in both hands.

"Mr. Rivers! What are you-"

I moved towards him. Before I could say Jack Robinson he had hurled Francis into the fire. He grabbed the fire poker and held Francis down, pressing him mercilessly down into the hot coals behind the grate.

I shrieked and grabbed the washbasin. I knew Francis to be relatively fire resistant, but this would surely be the end of him. Francis was struggling against the poker. I ran to throw the water on the fire but Rivers let go of the poker and grabbed me. The water sloshed over the two of us.

"There now, enough hysterics," he said in a calm but firm voice, the kind you'd use for a child who didn't want to go to bed. "Just look."

I was wet and angry and struggling to get out of his grip, but I couldn't help looking. And then I stopped struggling.

Francis was glowing. Not only did he seem unharmed by the fire, he seemed to be basking in it. He seemed to be part of it. And he was expanding. Even as we both watched, he pushed out of his skin. Compared to the intact skin he left behind, he was now a good quarter bigger, if that were possible.

"See?" Rivers murmured. "This is one of the things they didn't want you to know."

Francis climbed slowly out of the grate and looked at us. Then he rushed up the front of my skirts and clung to my forearm. I was surprised by how much heavier he felt. He gave Rivers a fixed stare of outrage for an instant, then stretched out his neck and bit him soundly on the arm.

Rivers let out a rather beautiful howl of indignation. Francis continued upwards to my shoulder and perched there protectively, facing Rivers, daring him to touch me again.

I burst out laughing. I couldn't help it, and I didn't help it. Rivers looked up for an instant from examining his wound.

"Hysterics again, Miss Worms?" he muttered.

"No, Mr Rivers, I'm laughing. I'm laughing at you," I said distinctly. He sneered, rolling down his shirt sleeve to cover the wound. "And now I'm going to have you removed from the estate. I've no wish to hear anything more you may have to say to me."

"Wait!" The panic in his voice surprised me so much that I paused. "I'm leaving tomorrow. Let me stay tonight."

"What! And have you creeping about the house all night?" I scoffed. "Or hiding in my bedroom again? I think not."

At this he took a key out of his pocket and presented it to me. "The key to my bedroom," he explained, with a self-satisfied air.

I recoiled. His eyes flicked to the ceiling in exasperation. "So you can be sure *I stay in it.*"

I hesitated. He thrust it at me again, impatiently. "Come now, I've ordered a carriage tomorrow after breakfast. I can hardly be sent alone across the moor tonight. Think how much trouble it will be for your cousin to eject me now, simply to gratify your wounded feelings. Are you really so selfish?"

I gritted my teeth. His words stung me because there was some truth in them. Gwendolyn had seemed unusually fragile today. Surely it would be best to do as he said and let him leave willingly and without a fuss in the morning?

I took the key and gestured to the door. He opened it and I marched him down the passage like a prisoner on the way to his cell. Once we got there I shut him in and locked it from the outside with great pleasure. Francis was still on my shoulder.

As an afterthought, I called through the door. "Do you need anything for the bite, Mr. Rivers?" I might enjoy locking him in his room but I didn't want to torture him.

"No. Members of the Varanidae family are not venomous, Miss Worms," he answered in weary tones. "I have all that I require."

"Do you really?" I muttered on my way back to my room. I myself was convinced that there were a great many things that Rivers required. First among them, a stint of unemployment, which I intended to make sure he got forthwith. I would write to Mother's cousin in the morning and tell him how highly unsatisfactory Rivers had been. But…what else would I tell him exactly? That I'd found a creature of near mythical powers? That Rivers had some sinister interest in it? That though I was convinced the man was a liar and a sneak, he was right that the household was full of secrets?

But that part was quite all right. Tomorrow would put me in Gwendolyn's confidence and restore to us all a Wormwood Abbey devoid of Rivers. And that, I imagined, would be a Paradise Restored.

CHAPTER TEN

The following day was Sunday. We had planned for the whole family to go to Divine Service at the village church, but George had a bad case of the sniffles brought on by lying on his front in a pond all afternoon watching a dragonfly perform its metamorphosis. We thought to leave George behind with the servants, but at the last minute Rivers's carriage was late to fetch him. I had unlocked the man's room at breakfast time, and I wasn't about to leave him at liberty in the house with the family gone to church.

In the fluster of getting everyone in the carriage, I told Mother I'd stay back to make sure George rested and didn't get up to mischief. Gwendolyn's eyes met mine and she gave me a small, serious nod. She knew exactly why I wanted to see Rivers safely off.

I felt a little flush of pleasure that we shared a secret together. Did this mean we were friends?

The house was now very quiet, and I liked it. As it was Sunday, I couldn't work on my novel. I have always observed a Sabbath rest from my literary labours, and I believe it does me good. I went up to the library with Francis to find the book Drake had reminded me of. I thought of the tapestry, but I could hardly investigate it until Rivers left.

I settled myself on the window seat contentedly while Francis poked about and ran along the tops of the shelves. The book crackled with age and disuse as I opened it to the frontispiece. It read as follows:

An Historical Relation of the Island CEYLON, in the EAST-INDIES: Together With an ACCOUNT of the Detaining in Captivity the Author and divers other Englishmen now Living there, and of the AUTHOR'S Miraculous ESCAPE. Illustrated with Figures, and a Map of the ISLAND. By ROBERT KNOX, a Captive there near Twenty Years. LONDON, Printed by Richard Chiswell, Printer to the ROYAL SOCIETY, at the Rose and Crown in St. Paul's Church-yard, 1681.

I CHORTLED. I ought to send that to my publisher next time he told me my titles were too long.

Lily came and told me when Rivers's hired carriage arrived for him. I did not go down to bid him goodbye. I had no desire to speak with the man ever again and I felt the greatest satisfaction at his prompt dismissal.

I had intended to go down to the tapestry but I found myself absolutely immersed in Knox's memoir of life in the Kingdom of Kandy as a prisoner of the Raja.

The son of the ship's captain, Knox had been ship-wrecked on the island in 1659 at only nineteen years of age. His prose was admirable, and he was liberally disposed towards the native peoples with whom he lived for twenty years, both of which made him a congenial guide. In my growing interest in Knox's adventures, I even forgot why I had picked it up in the first place. I couldn't wait to share this puritan Marco Polo with Father.

It was a good two hours before I thought to check on George, and even then I almost didn't do it at all, I am ashamed to say, as I found my reading matter so absorbing. And there was still the tapestry to investigate.

But I had told Mother I would, so I popped Francis back in my room with a bread-crust and went in search of him, even though I thought George could take care of himself. He wasn't in his room, so I wandered down to the kitchen. This was the most likely place to find him as the hour of mealtime drew nearer.

"Cook, have you seen my brother? He is supposed to be in bed with a cold, but he seems to be at large."

"We've seen nowt of him," she answered in her usual flat tones, wiping her hands on her apron. "But just come see this, Miss Edith."

She led me out the kitchen door into the yard and towards an outbuilding. She opened the door on a dark storeroom.

"Who's done that, then?" Cook pointed inside.

Pilot was tied up by a rope to an iron ring in the wall. He whined piteously and wagged his tail at us. I went to him and started on the knot immediately.

"I can't imagine," I said, appalled.

Just then I caught a glimpse of Pip across the yard. "Have you asked him?"

Cook shouted at the boy. "Pip! Where've tha been all morning? Come here, now, and answer the lady's questions, she's looking for Master George."

Pip took off his cap and twisted it in his hands.

"It's all right, Pip, only I'm supposed to be looking after my brother and I can't find him. Do you know where he might be?"

Pip swallowed. "He asked me for a tinderbox."

"Speak up, boy," said Cook. There was a harsh edge to her voice that I thought unnecessary.

"He asked me for a tinderbox and I got it for 'im. He never told me what for. But he had it in his mind, Miss."

"He had what in his mind?" I asked, my stomach tightening, though I didn't yet know why.

"Seeing the caves, Miss."

Cook put her hand over her mouth. I touched her arm.

"No, no, it's all right, Cook. I'm quite sure my brother wouldn't have been foolish enough to go into the caves alone."

"But he weren't alone, Miss."

Cook and I stared at him.

"He were goin' on a trake with that man from London, that Mr Rivers."

COOK HAD GONE OFF IMMEDIATELY with a grim face to find her husband, Thomas. She sent Pip to Drake Hall for reinforcements, exclaiming loud prayers to God all the while. I myself was saying silent ones as I untied Pilot.

All of a sudden it seemed clear that Rivers had planned this, and it was he who had tied up Pilot. Drake had said that Pilot would never allow George to go anywhere dangerous, and it seemed that somewhere dangerous was exactly where Rivers had wanted to go. But why take George with him? Who on earth would take a curious boy with him on a secretive and sinister errand? What help could George possibly provide?

Pilot took off instantly.

"Wait!" I cried. "Pilot!" Might there be some way of tracking George? Was Pilot already on his scent?

I ran after him out of the yard and found him nose

down in the grass. He barked at something there. I quickly caught up with him. It was George's cap. He was always losing it. Pilot barked at it again and then looked up at me, much agitated. Could he be tracking George already?

I picked up the cap and instinctively held it to Pilot's nose.

"George. Find him, Pilot. Help me find him."

I stared into the dog's enormous eyes as if I might find an intelligible answer there. He whirled round in a flurry of jowls, tongue and fur, and set off with unmistakable purpose. I seized the rope which was still trailing from his collar and trotted behind him. I realised he was taking me back the way Drake had walked with me. We were heading back to the hidden wood.

What if Pilot was just going back to Drake Hall to seek his master? My thoughts were spinning. But surely this must also be the way to the caves. Whether Pilot led me to the caves or the Hall, both would be better than remaining here, doing nothing. At the Hall I might find men to help in the search. If I stopped following Pilot now I might never know if he would have led me to George. And time must be of the essence in scenting his trail.

The two of us made an awkward, hasty descent of the hillside. It had certainly been easier with Drake to help me. What was it I'd said so disdainfully to myself about clinging ivy?

As soon as we reached the bottom we made better speed along the river path towards the Great Rock. We crossed the stepping stones together, and then I saw that Pilot was not taking me to Drake Hall after all. He veered left, continuing upriver. Every now and then he put his nose down as if tracing someone's route. I prayed it was George's.

As we drew close to the Great Rock I recognised my

surroundings. We were almost at that desolate ravine I had climbed down just yesterday. I felt an odd chill of dread as I reached the end of the wood. But of course this is where the caves were, in the ravine. Was that why I had sensed danger in the place? Might it even be the very place that my uncle and cousin had been found dead?

I had followed Pilot about halfway into the ravine when he swung behind a rock outcropping that was bigger than my body. I was now looking into the opaque black of a cave mouth. Pilot turned and panted at me as if he was waiting for instructions. I shouted into the blackness.

"George? George! Halloo? Are you in there? Is anybody in there?"

I waited, but heard nothing save for the birds in the wood behind us. I sat on a rock, feeling bleak.

"We must wait here for help, Pilot. I don't have a light. Someone must come to help us soon."

I thought of Drake, but he had gone to church in the village and it might be an hour or more before he knew anything was amiss.

Pilot wagged his tail, and barked into the cave. Then he sniffed the pebbles at our feet. He whimpered and looked at me. Then he pawed at George's cap, which I still held gripped in my hand. I knew without a doubt that he wanted me to go with him into the cave. That he wanted to take me to George.

"I can't, Pilot, it's not safe."

As soon as I'd said it, I knew that was why I had to go in. It wasn't safe. Rivers was not safe, and I had brought him to the Abbey. The caves were not safe, and I had not guarded my brother from them this morning.

If it wasn't safe for me to go in, how much less safe was it for George, who had gone in without Pilot, and with a man of few principles? Who knew what dreadful design

Rivers had in taking him there? He must have left the carriage further down the road and come back for George. He had made very sure that he would be undetected.

I could bear it no longer. I stood up and took a step into the shadow of the cave. Pilot took that as agreement and plunged in, pulling me after him.

The inky darkness closed over me. As I'd been standing in full sunlight a moment before, I was totally blinded. My other senses told me we were moving down a shingly slope, and the air was shockingly cold. It was strangely exhilarating, like plunging into a deep rock pool on a hot day.

Of course, it is exceedingly stupid, quite mad in fact, to run blindly into a dark cave. I can think of nothing stupider, and I beg you never to do it. Knowing what I now know, I don't think I could do it again.

But Pilot was leading me with absolute certainty. I felt that for the moment he was the master and I was the dumb beast. My eyes began to adjust but we had left the daylight behind us now. I threw a glance over my shoulder and saw only faint light from the entrance. I had no idea how big was the cavern I was moving through.

Now Pilot slowed. He put his nose down and sniffed again. As I waited in the quietness I could hear water. I could make out something, too. Good heavens, were there stars above me? I thought I saw a night sky adorned with strange constellations. My heart thudded in confusion.

"Glow worms!" I exclaimed. What a wondrous sight in this dark place. Somehow the creatures cheered me a little.

Pilot made a sharp turn, into a narrower place, and my heart quickened again. I made an effort to breathe deeply to calm myself. I was alone in an unmapped underground labyrinth. I, who got lost in broad daylight. I thought of Theseus and the magical ball of wool he had received from

Ariadne. I wished I had a magical ball of wool to unspool through these black chambers.

"But I do," I thought. His name is Pilot. I remembered Drake's voice: *He has seen me to safe harbour many a time.*

I whispered to him with a shaky laugh. "Just please, Pilot…please don't take me to the Minotaur." I refused to allow myself to think any more explicitly than that of the man-killing wolf pack I'd been told haunted the caves.

We now had to go more slowly, as the floor was uneven and occasionally slippery. The walls of this chamber were just a bit wider than my body, and smooth and damp. I had lost all hope of keeping count of the turns I had taken.

This was a dream. No. I focused on the feeling of the rope gripped in my cramped fingers and the cool air in my lungs. I must not lose my head.

I'd been conscious for a while now that we were approaching running water. Somehow this also cheered me. I remembered standing on the Great Rock in the sun with the larks above me and knowing that the river must run deep below me, in secret places under the Rock.

That was where I was now, with that very river. The river I had crossed with Drake. The river that flowed through the lovely Faerie wood. I told myself that this river would not, could not hurt me. Then I remembered that Faerie-land always shows a beautiful aspect to humans, until it traps them forever within its borders. And who could say what cruel beasts might lurk there?

"Stop," I told myself. I tried to focus on what I knew. By the sound of water, I predicted that any moment we must either turn a different way or cross the swift-running underground river. If I dared to cross it. I would have no way of knowing how deep or wide it was. This struck me as rather hard. And then a horrible new doubt pierced me: was it possible for Pilot to accurately track someone's scent through water? We had already crossed a river once. What if my faith in him was misplaced? I felt instantly sick.

I pictured Pilot in my head. I thought of the monks of the Alps in their mountain fastness, perfecting through centuries of breeding the enhanced senses God had given these Mastiffs of the Alps to find the lost and injured, despite the most inhospitable conditions. I must trust that between God, the monks of St. Bernard, and Pilot himself, I was in good hands.

There was light ahead! My heart gave a leap. It was only dim, but still it dazzled me a little. It was a shaft of light from a cleft in the rock above. I looked up, but I could not see the sky, only some ferns a very long way above me in the narrow shaft. But it was enough to show me the secret river flowing past.

Pilot began to swim across. I could not see how deep it was, but I was terrified to let go of the rope. I sat on the slippery edge and extended my legs downward as far as they could go. My boot was heavy with water and buffeted by the strong current but it touched the bottom. I launched myself into the current, gasping with the icy shock, trying not to slip, trying not to drag Pilot under the water by pulling at his rope. I thought of what it would be like to be carried away, deeper and deeper underground, away from that single shaft of light.

Pilot scrambled ashore on the other side. I threw myself onto the edge and dragged myself out most ungracefully, clinging to his rope, sodden and gasping. Pilot wagged his tail and licked me as if to show his approval of my efforts.

I gathered myself into a sitting position and breathed for a minute. Pilot clearly was itching to go on. I could hardly bring myself to leave the only bit of light and connection to the outside world I'd seen in…how long? I didn't know. Would a message have reached my family yet?

I thought of my Father, ruffling George's hair at the breakfast table. I thought of Mother, who had lost two children after George - one miscarried in the early months of tentative rejoicing, one born too soon and as soon buried.

I pulled myself to my feet, skirts clinging to my legs.

"All right, Pilot. Let's go get George."

I soon sensed that this passage was quite different from the others I'd traveled through. The floor was very even. The walls where my fingers brushed them felt as if they'd been hewn out of the rock with human tools. Oddly, this gave me hope. People had been here before. People might come again to look for me.

The passage widened out at last and I felt we were in a large chamber once again, perhaps larger than any I'd been in yet.

Suddenly the rope went slack. Pilot had stopped stock still. My soaked boots and skirts thudded into something that stopped me short. I lurched to a halt. It wasn't a rock. It was soft and firm, like a sack of something, or…

I reached out trembling hands and bent down. A lifeless body. Oh, God help me.

My aching hands felt along the arm. With a sob of relief, I discerned it was an adult arm. Then I felt a bandage was wrapped round it, near the wrist, which was devoid of a pulse. To clinch the matter, the hand was gripping a circular object that had a metallic rim and a shard of something that hurt me. Rivers.

Then I realised. I had let go of the rope. I now had no idea where Pilot was. I was Theseus, in the Labyrinth, with no magical guide, and at my feet there lay a victim of the Minotaur.

CHAPTER ELEVEN

At this terrifying moment, I heard the most welcome sound in the world: a human voice, from further off in the cavern.

"Hello? Is anyone there?" It was George, sounding terribly small and uncertain.

"George! George!" I cried out, and at the same time I knew Pilot had found him and was barking joyfully and panting and slobbering all over him. I stumbled towards them, tears hot on my face. The shingle underfoot was very flat and slippery here and with my wet skirts and uncertain footing it took me a moment to find them. I had abandoned all caution and would have certainly plummeted to my death if there had been any crevasses in the chamber.

"Eddie? Is that you?" I could tell from his voice that George was crying too. "I'm ever so sorry, Eddie, really I am…"

"Don't be an idiot!" I was holding him in my arms now. How small he was. Why had I never noticed how small he still was?

After a time I sat back on my heels. My hands were cramping horribly but I wrapped Pilot's rope around my wrist securely. I found my handkerchief and offered it to George.

"Now George, you will tell me all about this later. I'm going to ask Pilot to take us home now. But first, are you hurt? Can you walk?"

"I'm all right. I just lay down because I was so tired, and I knew when you're lost you're supposed to stay where you are until someone finds you."

"Quite right, old fellow."

"I must have fallen asleep. But Eddie, what about Mr. Rivers?"

I swallowed. I didn't know what George had been through. I simply didn't have the heart to say to him in the blackness, "The man who brought you in here is lying dead over there." I was ashamed of my momentary panic a few moments earlier. But still I had no idea how Rivers had died and how long his body had lain there near my brother in the dark.

"How did you get separated?" I asked instead.

"He told me to wait here. He…he took the candles I'd brought."

"What!"

"I asked him not to leave me but he said I was being a coward. He said he would come back at once. But he didn't come back. It was ever so long."

Perhaps I shouldn't have been angry with a man whose body was hardly cold, but I was. I was also very keen to get George safely out of this place where people died mysteriously for no apparent reason. Wasn't there something about poisonous gases underground that killed unwary explorers now and then?

I briefly thought of going through the man's pockets to

find the candles he'd taken from my brother, but now that I had my hands on both Pilot and George, I couldn't bear to let go of either of them.

"We can't help him by staying here in the dark, George."

That was true enough. The man was entirely past helping. I made my voice cheerier.

"Right. Just hold on to Pilot's rope, it's here. Ready to go?"

"Yes, well, almost." He seemed to be stuffing things into his pockets. Trust George to collect rocks at a time like this. "I'm ready."

Now came the moment I was counting on. I had no plan besides this one. Pray God it would work, or our fate might be the same as Rivers's.

"Home, Pilot. Take us home."

Pilot started moving instantly. Quite soon we were back in the passage which I believed was quarried by human hands. My spirits lifted. We were going to get out.

This part of the trip was far preferable to my mad dash into unknown terrors. I was with George. I had proof that Pilot could guide us reliably.

"What happened to your light? Did you drop it?" asked George.

"What light?"

"Eddie, you didn't come all this way without a light?" he asked in disbelief.

I laughed. "Yes, I did, and I hope you never do anything as stupid as that in your whole life. Pilot brought me the whole way. Drake said he would keep you safe, remember? Why on earth did you tie him up?"

"Tie him up? But I didn't! Mr. Rivers said Pilot was with Mr. Drake."

"Let's not talk about Rivers now."

We had got to the shaft of sunlight now. The water was just as icy but at least I knew how deep it was this time. George forded the river nimbly. I began to feel almost cheerful.

The next part of the journey was the longest. We went a little slower now we weren't following George's trail. Pilot seemed just as certain about the way out as he had about the way in.

"I don't know how you did it," George would say in wonder. "I keep bashing into rocks. And I'm not wearing those beastly flopping things you have to wear. I don't know how the Greeks managed to conquer the world in skirts."

"Oh, I dare say we'll be absolutely black and blue when we see ourselves in the light of day," I said cheerily. "Maybe you'll even have some lovely scars. As for the Greeks, I think they were mostly naked."

"Are we going the right way do you think? Rivers - I mean, we had some sort of map coming in, besides a light."

A map! Of course. But how on earth had he come by a map of these caves, which Gwendolyn had warned me were unexplored? I forced myself to focus on the present task.

"I have the greatest possible faith in Pilot. But this part is the longest, and the most tedious, because the ground's so slippery."

I realised that George had been in the dark even longer than I, and though the little fellow had put a brave face on it, he was still a child. A child who'd been abandoned in a cave by a man he must have trusted. I was thankful he didn't know about the wolves that savaged his uncle and cousin, perhaps in these very chambers.

"Why don't we sing?"

We sang the Doxology a few times, laughing a bit over the line *all creatures here below*. Then we sang 'Marlborough Has Gone to Battle.' This did the trick nicely. I found it impossible to think of wolves leaping on me in the darkness when loudly singing a nursery song.

"Edith, look!" George's voice was very excited. The strange stars were above us again.

"Praise be to God, the glow worms! Praise Him, all creatures here below. I saw them on the way in, George! That means we're almost at the entrance!"

"I didn't see them on the way in, because of our light, I suppose. Could we stay and look at them for a bit?" he asked wistfully.

God bless the child. "No, George, we couldn't," I said firmly.

A bit further on and we heard a shout ahead of us and saw faint light growing ahead and above us as we neared the entrance.

"Hallooooo!" we shouted together. "We're all right! I found him! We're both here!"

As soon as we scrambled up the slope into blinding sunlight I suddenly felt terribly weak and floppy and dreamlike. I sank to the ground.

I couldn't see very well in the dazzling sunlight, but right away there were arms supporting me and a gentle hand unwinding Pilot's rope from my wrist. I saw my hand was bleeding from where I'd grasped Rivers's shattered eye glass.

There were a lot of people with ropes and lanterns and rifles and even a rope ladder. I could hear Mother crying but it was a happy sound. I'd heard her cry over the two babies who were lost. It had not sounded like this.

Someone put a flask to my lips and I thought it was water so I gulped it.

"Brandy," said a low voice in my ear, an instant too late. The brandy burned my throat horribly but somehow it also helped me think and see more clearly. I was no longer drifting away.

Now Father was with me, kissing my forehead and embracing me and thanking me and telling me to promise I would never do something so foolish again. To which I willingly assented.

So whoever had helped me before hadn't been Father but someone else. I looked around to thank him. Suddenly I heard people asking about Rivers. It was time for me to speak.

"Rivers is dead." I tried to speak strongly but I think my voice trembled a bit.

There was an instant hush over the group. George stared at me from Mother's arms.

"I found his body, not far from you. I'm sorry, George, I couldn't bring myself to tell you, in there."

I spotted Drake then. He was kneeling not far from me, with Pilot. He stood up.

"We should take them to the Hall. It's nearer than the Abbey."

I looked at him in surprise. "But…won't you go and get his body?"

Drake looked away, then back at me.

"You are absolutely certain he was dead?"

I nodded. "Quite certain."

"Then he is beyond help."

The group of rescuers was already gathering up their things to go.

I put a hand on Drake's arm.

"But surely, a Christian burial…his family…"

He turned and spoke almost harshly to me now.

"These farmers and shepherds also have families, Miss

Worms. Your rescue of your brother was well-nigh miraculous. Can you guarantee another miracle? If any of these men are lost to the caves, will you be the one to tell their wives and children?"

I drew back, startled by the darkness of his face and tone. Had I really thought his face a kind one only yesterday?

We were taken slowly to the Hall. The wood was bright and green. I felt like days and nights were all mixed up.

Mother tenderly bathed and bandaged our wounds and we were given fresh clothes which a servant brought from the Abbey.

Then we went down to the sitting room and had tea and toast and seedcake, which George ate indecent quantities of, to our parents' delight. I suppose there's nothing like eating seedcake to prove one is alive and relatively unscarred.

Drake Hall proved to be an elegant Elizabethan gentleman's residence, small but perfectly formed, tucked among the trees within sight of the river and the Great Rock. We could not see the fells from it at all. Instead, from the upper room where I changed, I glimpsed a waterfall through the foliage of ash and alder that whispered about the walls.

It was a charming place, not at all what I'd imagined, completely lacking the gothic atmosphere of Wormwood Abbey. The sitting room had a bright fire and panelled walls carved with fruit and birds. The pictures were all very good, and the blue and white china cups showed to advantage against the panelling. It had the feeling of a snug ship's cabin during a storm, or a peaceful haven after one. All was well-made and well chosen, with no ostentation. I wondered who had chosen it all. I'd never heard anything about any other Drakes, but this didn't feel like the home of a lonely bachelor.

I thought this would make a nice change for Gwendolyn, if everything could be arranged between her and Drake. At this moment, I preferred the house to the man, and I sincerely wished Gwendolyn joy of them both.

It was here in the panelled sitting room, with Pilot resting on the rug at his feet, that George told Drake and our parents his story. It went like this:

George had been keen to make friends with Rivers as soon as he found out the man was a naturalist, but Rivers had given him very little encouragement. The day he'd been dismissed that changed. (The dismissal came as a surprise to George, whom no one had thought to tell— George had been face down in a dragonfly pond all that day.) Rivers showed him a few of his notebooks and looked over George's own collections with apparent respect.

Then he told George about an aged document: a mysterious map, which he claimed to have found in the papers of a descendant of Sir Francis Drake's secretary. He told the story of a legendary treasure looted from the Spanish during the time of Elizabeth and hidden in a Yorkshire cave. He told it in quite an off-hand way, as if it was simply a story. George very excitedly put two and two together, having heard from Drake their family connection to the privateer. Rivers had responded doubtfully at first, feigning to be gradually persuaded that the cave here in the Dale might be the one the map pertained to. Rivers had kept a copy of the treasure map in his notebook, apparently quite by chance.

Together, they had hatched a plan to test out the theory on the following day while the family was at church. This was the part of the story George was most ashamed of. He was not a dishonest child, but he had allowed himself to be talked into doing something he knew was forbidden.

At this point, George's eyes became fixed on the rug.

His cap, which had been restored to him, was in his lap and he twisted the rim of it in his hands.

"You see, Rivers told me the Estate was in trouble. And…well, *we're* all right, but it seems so beastly for Gwendolyn and the girls. I thought if we found the treasure, everything could be put right."

"Don't be hard on yourself, George," I said crisply, putting my tea cup down. "I had a run in with Rivers myself, and he was rather slippery. I'm not proud of how I handled him myself, and I'm not eleven years old."

He flashed me a look of gratitude. He went on to tell of the foray into the caves. I was still completely puzzled as to why Rivers had taken him there, but this didn't seem to trouble George. I suppose he'd read enough G.A. Henty books to assume that the boy is always in the middle of the adventure.

"Then, when we'd got to the treasure chamber, he told me to give him my candles and wait for him. I didn't want to be left alone in the dark." His voice was very small now. "I asked him not to leave me, but he told me I was…I was a disgrace to the Empire. So I tried to be brave and wait. He went away down one of the passages. I thought it would help me keep track of how long I'd been there if I counted in my head, but I kept losing count."

Father's face was very pale now. Mother was clasping her hands together in her lap.

"And he didn't come back. At least, I thought he didn't. I called out for a while, but I didn't hear anything. Everyone always says if you're lost you should stay still. So I did. I must have fallen asleep, because I didn't hear Edith come in at first. But then I heard something and I started to yell like the dickens. Wasn't I surprised when Edith answered! I'm ever so sorry, Father. About everything."

"George," Father spoke quietly. "I owe you an apology."

"Whatever for, sir?"

"I perceived that Rivers was not a principled man, but I thought it was exigent to allow him to assist us in legal matters. I should have dismissed him the moment he acted rudely towards your sister."

I looked up in surprise. Father was still white-faced.

"And for that I owe you an apology also, Edith."

"Well, now, Father, don't excite yourself," I answered, with a spark of mischief. "You'll never build the Empire that way you know."

Drake burst out laughing. We all looked at him in astonishment. His laugh was as startling as his smile had been. He turned away to master himself.

"Forgive me," he murmured.

"Mr. Drake, at a time like this," said Father, "laughter is not merely a pleasure, but a service to others."

Mother patted Father on the arm appreciatively.

"You'll have to work that into one of your sermons, dear. *A merry heart doeth good like medicine,* that's your text."

"But I don't understand how Mr. Rivers…how he died," George faltered over the words.

"Perhaps he had a weak heart, dear," said Mother. She always had such sane explanations for things. Of course, he must have taken fright at something. Perhaps his light had gone out suddenly. I had felt rather shabby myself at several points, and if anyone had a strong heart, it was me.

George was looking a bit sick and fingering his cap again.

"I—I called him a beast. When he didn't come back after a while. When I was shouting after him. What if he was lying there, dying, and he heard me?"

Father answered firmly. "If he did, we can hope that

perhaps it caused him to regret his evil deeds and to call out for mercy to the one Who must shortly judge him."

George looked serious but a little less ill. He took a deep breath and turned to Drake.

"Mr. Drake, I heard you tell my sister the farmers would be afraid to get Mr. Rivers out."

Drake listened to George attentively.

George's eyes were bright now. "Would it make any difference if they knew about the treasure? I'm sure we could share it with them."

Oh, the dear boy. We all exchanged a glance. Nobody wanted to say it.

"George," I began, tackling the unpleasant task at once. "I'm afraid there isn't any treasure. I've no idea why Rivers dragged you in there, but I feel sure he had some other purpose of his own and simply made up the treasure as something that would appeal to you."

George blinked.

"Edith, what are you talking about? Of course there's treasure. Didn't you see it?"

"See it?"

"Oh, of course, you didn't have a light, I forgot. That's all right, I brought some out with me."

Then the boy kneeled down on the floor and upended his cap in front of him.

Something heavy spilled out of it, making a faint ringing tone as it did so, and settled itself into a dull golden pile on the rug. It glowed in the light of the fire. The sound recalled a memory, and now I saw that it wasn't rocks that George had stopped to fill his pockets with before we made our escape from the caves. It was coins.

There was a moment of complete silence. Then Father said, "I think I'd like another cup of tea now, Emily."

CHAPTER TWELVE

Gwendolyn startled me by clasping me in a fierce, quick embrace the moment I got back to the Abbey. Then she drew back and scrutinised me. "You're not hurt?"

I was warmed by her concern. "Just a few cuts and scratches. I know I'll wake up with a hundred aches and pains, but right now all I want is to go to bed."

She nodded, then gripped my arm for an instant. "Tomorrow."

A few minutes later I was in my room contemplating falling into bed fully dressed when Mother came in.

"I thought you might like help," she said. I nodded gratefully and turned round for her to unfasten the buttons of my dress.

"Edith, my dear…"

"It's all right, Mother, you don't have to thank me," I said rather lightly. I felt tears prickling at my eyelids. "I'd never have been able to face you and Father again if I hadn't gone after George."

"But that's exactly why I have to speak to you." She

gently turned me round to face her. "I don't want to thank you for saving George. I want you to know that it means just as much to me that *you* came out of that dreadful place alive as he did."

All of a sudden I was sobbing like a child. We sat on the bed together and she put her arms around me. I felt as if some buried pain deep inside me had been laid bare and at the same time, healed.

Mother hushed me and kissed me on the top of my head, exactly as if I was her fair-haired boy, and not a red-headed stepdaughter at all.

Then she finished helping me out of my things, tucked me in bed, and left the room. I was already drifting off to sleep, curled up on my side like a child, when I sensed Francis climb onto the coverlet and nestle into the hollow at the back of my knees. It felt strangely comforting. I remembered him biting Rivers, and instead of the memory disturbing me, it made me feel safe.

I WOKE VERY EARLY next day. My mind seemed to have an unusually crystalline clarity. Since I had come to the Abbey I'd been surrounded by half-truths and secrets, I was certain. What kind of a detective novelist was I if I couldn't get anywhere with my own family's mystery? It occurred to me that up to this point I'd been behaving entirely too much like one of my doomed damsels who, though undoubtedly plucky and virtuous, mostly required Green's cunning and wisdom to get them out of their predicaments.

What was it Gwendolyn had said about my inspector? That he would make everything all right at the end? It came home to me all of a sudden that I *could* bring Inspector Green here to look at all the clues and speak to all the witnesses. Because, after all, the Inspector's only existence was in my head, whatever Gwendolyn might think.

Gwendolyn had promised to meet me with Drake today and bring me entirely into her confidence. But, upon reflection, I couldn't quite believe her. Every time she had been close to confiding in me, I had asked the wrong question (or perhaps the right one) and her defences had gone up instantly. A lifetime of secrecy had shaped her. How could I expect this time to be different?

Drake, on the other hand, was a different kettle of fish. He had seemed to be on the cusp of telling me something several times. Each time he had stopped himself. He clearly wanted me to solve the puzzle myself.

Well, I was going to solve as much of it as I could. And I had until tea-time.

"All right, then, Inspector," I said aloud to the room. "You and I are going to make an end of all this nonsense."

It was just after tea when Gwendolyn and Drake knocked on my study door. I had spent a reasonably informative day. My plan now was to use the limited information I had uncovered to convince them that I knew more than I did, so they would be surprised into giving away more than they intended.

"Come in," I said, with a ring of authority, despite my quickening heart.

I saw with satisfaction that they blinked a little in surprise when the door opened. I had spent a quarter of an hour rearranging the room for this meeting. The after-noon light flowing in through the tower windows struck them in the face. I had my back to the light, and I was seated with Francis on my lap. Francis had definitely grown again, and added to the confident air I intended to convey. I had chosen a chair that elevated me slightly above them. They were left to sit on the low ladies' chairs set before me. Drake had to fold his legs awkwardly to sit in one.

"Gwendolyn has promised me that the two of you will confide completely in me," I began.

They exchanged glances. Gwendolyn stammered. "Yes, of course, I did promise, and we will…but first…"

She looked at Drake with imploring eyes.

He followed his cue. He spoke with a heavy, stilted voice, as if he'd rehearsed his words and didn't much like them. "If you wish to know the secrets of the Abbey, Miss Worms, you must first bind yourself by taking the Ormdale Oath."

Well, this floored me.

"The *Ormdale Oath*?" I must have communicated by my tone how utterly absurd I found this because they both looked up at me, squinting a little against the light.

Drake carefully took an object from his coat pocket. It was about the size of a prayer book and wrapped in dark cloth. I regained my composure quickly. I had the upper hand and I did not mean to lose it now.

"Please give me the object, Mr Drake," I instructed.

Drake unwrapped it and handed it to me. I caught my breath. It was a highly decorated object of ivory, gold, and lapis, and studded with gems, exceedingly fine and of great antiquity. It appeared to be a small, flattish casket, similar to a jewellery box. I knew immediately what it was.

"And what exactly do you believe this to be?" I asked after holding it for a moment.

"I believe it to be a reliquary," answered Drake in slightly uncertain tones.

"Yes. That much is obvious. But what is the relic that you are asking me to swear upon?"

Drake looked blank. Gwendolyn looked back and forth between us. Things were clearly not going as they'd expected.

"Is it a piece of the True Cross? St. Brigid's wrist bone? No, it's too small. Wait—oughtn't it to be something more apropos? Let me see… A fragment of St. George's lance?"

Drake and Gwendolyn were now very pale indeed.

Drake cleared his throat. "We took the oath when we were children. We were not told what was inside it," he said at last, sounding a little defensive.

I almost lost heart then, in my pity for them. But I pressed on.

"You were coerced into swearing an oath of secrecy as children? And now you wish to impose this oath on me as well? Is that honourable, Mr. Drake?"

Drake looked down. I was growing angry now, though not with them.

"All right. This is what I shall do. I'll swear the Ormdale Oath." They both looked at me in astonishment. "If, and only if, you can tell me why I should."

My words fell on them like a crack of lightning.

"Why?" repeated Drake. Gwendolyn's mouth fell open slightly.

"Yes. Why?" I repeated. "I possess a fully formed mind and conscience, and to demand that I take an oath which incurs unknown burdens and calls down unknown calami-ties on my head is, to be frank, quite immoral. Though perhaps a little less immoral than it was to inflict it upon innocent children who were under an obligation to obey their elders."

Gwendolyn was looking at me in awe. It was then that Drake did something I had not foreseen at all. He laughed. I quickly realised that this was not the laughter of high spirits—it had a bitterness in it which was painful to hear.

"Simon?" implored Gwendolyn, putting her hand on his arm.

"Excuse me," he said. And left the room.

Oh, dear. I hadn't expected Green's methods to be quite so dramatic. On the other hand, Gwendolyn was still here, and she was my chief object after all.

I waited to see her response. She seemed in a bit of a daze. "Eleven years. I swore the Oath when I was ten years old. And I never asked why in eleven years," she said, rubbing her temples. "Do you—do you really think it was what you said? Immoral?"

"I do," I answered bluntly. "I'm sorry to say it of those who have passed away and cannot defend their actions. But I daresay they had the same thing done to them and perhaps that is some explanation."

"Yes," she said. "Father made all of us swear it. Una was only last year. Do you suppose there's something wrong with us? Generations of us, never asking why."

My heart was fairly wrung for her, but I had something important I needed to know. "Gwendolyn, I've something I need answered right away."

She looked up wearily at me. "What is it? I'll tell you, whatever it is. I owe you that."

"The venom that Francis has. The venom—it must have been what killed Rivers. Is there a treatment, or an antidote? A reliable one?"

She looked at me a little oddly. "Yes."

"And you have it here, at the Abbey? And it's effective?"

"Yes, we have it here. It's quite effective if applied straightaway."

I breathed a sigh of pure relief. I'd been keeping one hand on Francis throughout the conversation and now I released him. "Oh, I'm so glad. I was so worried I'd have to have him destroyed." I looked down at him, my eyes welling up. "I couldn't have him running about biting people when his bites can kill. And I've grown rather fond of him, quite apart from him being so special."

"It's not Francis you have to worry about," she said in a thick voice. "It's all the others."

A chill ran through me. "The others?"

CHAPTER THIRTEEN

I will now go back a little to help you understand what next I learned.

Early on the morning of that day, before the meeting with Drake and Gwendolyn in the tower room which I have described, I had crept quietly down to the Great Hall and there, in the pale morning light, I had finally looked behind the tapestries.

At first I was bewildered to find the wall perfectly solid, though a bit flaky with ancient plaster. There was no secret door, there was not even a loose stone behind which something might be hidden. The reverse of the tapestry itself proved equally unhelpful. I had thought perhaps there had been a map on it which had guided Rivers to the treasure. If so, he had removed it. I was about to give up when I realised that the stones were an odd colour. In fact, they were many different colours. It dawned on me that the wall had been painted with a design. The part I was currently looking at was very faded, and I must have examined the other parts too closely to perceive the pattern.

I climbed up on the oaken settle and removed the poles

from which the tapestries were hung. This took me a little time, and I was sneezing from all the dust. I felt sure the tapestries had not been beaten that spring and I thought I ought to have a word with Lily about that.

Once I had laid them all down on the floor, I was able to step back and get the full effect of the fresco. I immediately felt their artistic power and mourned the sections that were damaged. "They ought to be restored," I found myself saying, and then remembered how I had smiled at Mother for saying the same thing about the herb garden.

From what I could make out, they told an allegorical story of the Abbey's origin. The first pictures I could make out seemed to be portraying the pre-Christian conditions of Dale society. This was signified by people worshiping serpents, some of them winged or double-headed, and throwing smaller people to the creatures, presumably to be devoured (the medievals really didn't know how to draw children, did they?). Then the monks arrived, carrying crucifixes and a casket which likely contained a saint's relics. The serpents cowered in fear. I assumed this depicted the triumph of Christianity over Paganism. After that there was a section which was completely lost. Finally, I could make out somebody seated in an ornate chair (probably the Abbot by his garb) with a winged creature crouched beneath him. He was resting his foot on the beast's head.

"Well, that's hubris for you," I said to the image. "It's Christ who crushes the dragon's head, my dear Abbot."

There were many reasons why one might want to hide such an artwork. To preserve it from the bleaching effects of the sun, for instance, or to keep from alarming one's guests with images of human sacrifice. The Abbot's display of arrogance might be another reason.

What I most wanted to know was why Rivers had

found the fresco so enlightening. I remembered that he had only seen one section and by lamplight. I tried to retrace his steps to determine which section he had seen that night. Finally, I gave up. Whatever it was that had elicited that sound of triumph from him, only he knew, and he had carried that secret to the dark cave he had died in.

"THE OTHERS?" I repeated to Gwendolyn, trying to keep the chill I felt out of my voice.

"The ones that killed my father and brother."

The scenes from the fresco I had examined that morning flashed upon my mind, but this time I saw them not as faded pictures, but as the flesh and blood events that must have inspired them. Real monks, carrying a reliquary that I had seen in this very room. Real children being thrown to...to what, exactly?

"Dragons," I breathed.

Real dragons. I thought of the stone creatures that guarded the door to the Great Hall, the monstrous gargoyles on the ruined part of the Abbey. The silver, patterned with serpents. The library of bestiaries, including the one that provided directions on how to feed dragons.

And finally, I thought of the dragon which even now sat in my lap.

All of the clues, laid out for me, down to the very name I myself bore.

"Yes, God help us," said Gwendolyn. "Dragons."

We were silent for a moment. I looked down at the strong scaled body in my lap, flecked black and yellow. His blue forked tongue flickered in and out. Was this the kind of creature that St. George had fought? Would he grow to the size of a sailing ship?

There were too many questions to ask, but I had to start somewhere. "Why haven't I seen them? Why have I only seen Francis?"

"It's not the right time of year."

This answer was so banal that I stared at her. Could there be a season for mythical creatures, much as there was for ducks and pheasants?

"They hibernate," she went on. "You must have woken Francis up, or hatched him, more likely. You said he was in a log? He was probably still in his egg. His kind hatch with fire. I heard a story once about one of our old cooks, decades ago, who boiled a whole dozen thinking they were goose eggs and then came back to a kitchen full of dragons. From the size he was when I first saw him here, I'd guess he was a hatchling."

His kind? "How many of them…how many other kinds are there?" I wasn't sure I really wanted this question answered, but I needed it answered.

She passed a hand over her face; a gesture of exhaustion. "I don't know. I don't think anyone knows."

This horrified me a little, as she knew it would, I suppose. "And all the others are hibernating now?"

"Yes."

"What about the ones that killed your father and brother?" My heart rate quickened considerably. "Gwendolyn, is my family in danger right now?"

"No. I told you…at least, I told you half of the truth. Father and Percy went after them."

"But why?"

"The treasure," she said flatly. "The Drake treasure. Simon wouldn't have anything to do with it. He told them it was just a legend and begged them not to go. Those caves are dangerous, even without waking up things best left asleep. But Father was desperate. He said the estate couldn't go on. And Percy…well, Percy was always so hot-headed. He called Simon and me 'a pair of women.'" She swallowed down the memory, as if it stung her still. "They must have roused some of the beasts from their winter sleep by accident. They didn't have a map, like Rivers. God knows how he did. We never knew there was one."

She paused a moment and then went on. "When they didn't come back, Simon took Pilot and some of the farmers. They found their bodies, just as I told you. I didn't want to lie to you, Edith. I hoped…that someone…that one of you, might join us. But I was afraid that you wouldn't. Who would, if they had a choice? You're quite right about our parents. They made us take the oath as children so that we wouldn't dream of any other life. So that we'd be bound to this place forever."

I touched her hand. "Gwendolyn, you mustn't consider yourself bound by that oath. You had no choice."

"I've never had a choice. Not a single one." She said this with such bleak finality that I wanted to shake her. I restrained myself. She must be given time, and so must I.

"I have many more questions. Many!" I said. "But I think it's time we saw what's inside this, if there is anything at all. I'm going to try to open it, if you don't mind."

She nodded. I put Francis down, rather more carefully than usual. He climbed up to the window sill to catch the light.

There was a pair of my gloves on the desk. I put them on and sat down near Gwendolyn. I had seen my father handle historical documents before and I was convinced the reliquary was of genuine antiquity, whatever disreputable role it had played in ensuring the silence of my family members. "Do you know how it opens?" She shook her head. Gently, I felt the reliquary for a way to open it.

Gwendolyn suddenly pointed at a change in the pattern on one side. "What about here?"

I touched it and found a catch that delicately released the lid. I opened it very slowly, hardly daring to breathe.

Inside was a recess with something that had crumbled almost to powder. A few tiny shreds showed us it had once been a textile. But lying upon it like a jewel in a casket was something that had survived, something metallic. It was heavily tarnished, but quite recognisable.

"Good heavens." I kept my voice light. I felt almost dizzy. "Well, I think I made a pretty close guess."

Gwendolyn looked at me. "Is it…mail? I mean, chain-mail…like knights wore? Could it be…his? Or would that be too old?" she whispered.

I reflected. "The person you are speaking of was supposed to have died in the 4th century, I think. I've seen pottery older than that, not to mention coins. So if you're asking could this have lasted that long… Yes."

I sat back and looked over at Francis, my venomous pet dragon, basking on the hearthrug like a cat.

"Why not? If dragons are real, why shouldn't the story of St. George fighting one be real, too?"

I shut the reliquary softly and handed it back to Gwendolyn. She re-wrapped it in the cloth. After a moment she spoke wistfully.

"I'm not educated like you."

I didn't know how to answer this, so I didn't. She kept talking.

"My father…he wasn't like yours. He didn't think women needed much education."

I swallowed my indignation. I tried to say something polite instead of the rude things I wanted to say about my uncle. "How were you educated?"

"Hardly at all. Of course there was always the library, but I found those books so difficult whenever I tried them."

This was not a surprising sentiment about a library stuffed with medieval bestiaries and Anglo-Saxon poetry.

"Did you never have a governess?"

"Twice. But they were quite decrepit. I think Father chose them for their poor eyesight and antique ideas. One of them used to talk about the good old days before Queen Victoria came to the throne. Can you imagine? And she used to make us do elocution, endlessly. "

We shared a smile. I cleared my throat. "Gwendolyn, talking of my father… seeing as he is the heir presumptive or whatever of Wormwood Abbey, can't you see he ought to be told? About everything? I mean, he must have known once, but he has always told me his childhood seemed like a dream; half-real and half-imagined."

She looked like a deer that was deciding whether to bolt or not from the hand that reached to gentle it.

"What will he do?" she asked after a moment, her voice very strained.

"Truly, I haven't the faintest idea. But he's a good man. I don't know a better one. And he has the right to know."

I felt she was close to her breaking point. I shouldn't expect her to move quickly after all these years of secrecy and strain.

"I'll wait," I said. "You've had a number of shocks, as have I. I'll wait until you are ready."

She looked surprised. I was surprised myself. I had started this confrontation determined to gain the upper hand, but now that I did, I found I could not press my advantage. So many times I had felt like a schoolgirl under Gwendolyn's effortless bearing of authority. Now our positions were reversed. She had risked much to be honest with me and I felt I, too, should risk something.

"Now, let's go, or we'll be missed at tea," I said.

ONLY THE NEXT DAY, the strength of my promise to wait for Gwendolyn's decision was tested.

I made my way up to the library to meet Father and Mother, as per our standing arrangement. Yesterday it had been deferred, and I was assumed to be resting from my ordeals. As you have seen, I did no such thing, but I made up for it by lying in bed for hours the next morning with Knox's memoir of Ceylon while Francis tore apart an old and evidently unloved doll of Violet's which she had donated expressly for that purpose.

I found so many extraordinary things in that old volume. The Kingdom of Kandy was populated with creatures and customs completely unknown to me; even a mystical priesthood that worshiped in The Temple of the Tooth.

I looked at Francis and I began to wonder why I had ever thought I lived in a world *without* dragons.

Truly, Mother was right. The world has not emptied of mythos. It is we who have grown empty, and dull to its wonders.

When I arrived I saw that Gwendolyn was there with Mother on the window seat. She startled a bit when she saw me. She seemed to assume this was some kind of ambush. But as desperate as I was to talk to Father about all of this, I had remained faithful to my promise.

Father was tidying some papers at the desk and looked up brightly when I came in. "Ah, Edith, my dear. Here you are! I was afraid you mightn't feel up to it today."

"I'm perfectly rested, Father," I assured him, giving him a kiss on the cheek.

He pulled up a chair for me to sit in. "Now, we asked

both of you here to have a talk," he said, seating himself. "Emily and I had planned to do this before now, but we've had quite an eventful few days, haven't we? Now all the mysteries are over, or most of them at least, we'd like to talk about the future."

Gwendolyn swallowed. "The future?"

"Yes, of the Abbey, and our family." Father seemed rather cheerful, by which I hoped Gwendolyn would perceive that he wasn't talking about blood oaths and man-eating dragons. Of course, I had no idea what had made *her* father cheerful before tea, so perhaps not. He sounded a nasty piece of work to me.

"It seems the....various solicitors we have consulted are both right and wrong. The entail can't be broken—yet," explained my father.

Gwendolyn started breathing again. I suppose she could see they were only talking about her ordinary problems, not the ones that went bump in the night.

"We are advised that the time to break it is when George is of age, or when he marries, whichever comes first. It is at that time we have the chance to make some changes to how things are done. Indeed, I am advised that there is a great desire in this country to alter the laws of entail—or fee-tail, as our ancestors called it in former times. So waiting seems to be the very best thing we can do. There is hope that George may be able to settle an annuity on you and your sisters at that time, and perhaps on Edith, too, if she isn't supporting us all in luxury herself by then."

Father, in his cheeriness, was referring hyperbolically to the income I made from my novels, of which he had forgotten that Gwendolyn knew nothing. I squinted at him, which went unnoticed.

"But the question that faces us now, of course, is what

would be best for you and your sisters in the ten years that remain to us before George comes of age." At this, he paused. Mother took over seamlessly (I'm always impressed when they do that).

"We had a bit of trouble over this until George found his ridiculous pirate treasure. We've talked it over with Mr. Drake and he is insistent that the gold George brought out with him, being found on the Worms estate—it's the river apparently, Edith, that is the boundary between the estates, Gwendolyn will already know this—well, he's very insistent it must remain with this family."

Gwendolyn was, I could tell, quite confused, but I was following everything with great interest.

"But is it enough?" I broke in rather abruptly.

Gwendolyn looked at me. "Enough for what?" she asked.

Mother took over again. "That is for you to decide, Gwendolyn. It is enough to set the estate on a much better footing, with some hope of making it profitable in the future, if changes are made. Or, should you wish it, to set you and your sisters up elsewhere, in an entirely new household. Though of course, nothing of the scale you have been used to."

I thought for a moment that Gwendolyn was going to faint. She had gone white and was blinking fast. Mother turned to Father.

"George, dear, I think Gwendolyn might like a glass of water, or perhaps something stronger?"

Father disappeared briefly and returned with brandy. I was rather surprised that brandy was so near the library, but I suppose people needed to be roused from shocks everywhere in this house.

The brandy was administered. Gwendolyn, I saw, did not gulp it like I had done. Clearly she was more accustomed to both shocks and brandy than I. After she regained her composure, we went over the whole thing again, just to make sure she understood.

"But if I take the money for my sisters, won't I be… stealing from the estate in a way?"

Father paused, then answered her very kindly. "My dear, it appears obvious to Emily and I that you have been acting as an unpaid housekeeper and estate manager for your father for some time. In my way of thinking, you would be taking compensation for that. Of course, if it suited you better, you could treat it as a loan against the annuity that George will settle on you three in the future."

Gwendolyn looked back and forth between the three of us. "But if I don't take it, the money…it might…you think the money could really save the estate?"

"It's possible. If someone experienced is employed to take over the running of the estate right away…our opinion is that there is hope."

Gwendolyn took a long breath. "I see. So really, I'm choosing whether to put your son in my position, or even worse, in ten years' time, or to set the estate back on its feet."

I reminded myself never to underestimate Gwendolyn. She had a mind as sharp as a scalpel. Father and Mother exchanged glances.

All of a sudden, Gwendolyn was very calm. "Thank you very much, Uncle George and Aunt Emily. You have been very kind. But it seems quite impossible to make a choice that would run the estate into further ruin. I am grateful for your guidance. It seems that we are still left with the problem of supporting myself and my sisters, when all is said and done. Perhaps I can continue acting as housekeeper for the estate in return for a small stipend sufficient for my needs and those of my sisters."

Gwendolyn was now every inch the gentlewoman I had met at the entrance to Wormwood Abbey. This speech must have cost her dearly. I wanted to hug her, but I didn't dare.

Mother looked at Father and gave a little nod.

"There is another possibility which remains to you, my dear," offered Father.

Mother now smiled warmly at Gwendolyn.

"My dear niece, we keep a small household, quite unlike the Abbey, but it is comfortable and happy, as I'm sure Edith will tell you. I wish from the bottom of my heart to extend a welcome to all of my nieces to make a home there."

Gwendolyn's face went very still, but I knew her better than I used to, and I could read something in it I'd seldom seen there: hope.

Then it died. She looked down. Her lips twisted a little. "Aunt Emily, if you are sincere—and I think you must be as you are so good—I will gladly accept your offer…for my sisters. Una has grown much attached to you. Violet is exactly at the age when a mother's influence is most needed. I felt the lack of it myself at that age. But I must stay here." She said this in a voice that did not ask for pity, but still I felt as if she was reading out her own death sentence. "Whoever is to manage the estate may need my help. If I may ask it, I would like whoever you employ to be someone from the Dale. It would make things so much easier for the farmers. They don't take easily to outsiders."

I wanted to hug her, and I wanted to wring her neck.

Mother's cheeks were a little pink. I could see she was moved by Gwendolyn's attitude—and perhaps a little disappointed.

"You are doing a great service, my dear. But please, be sure it is worth the cost."

Gwendolyn inclined her head to acknowledge these words and then excused herself and left the room.

How much I wanted to tell my parents everything! But I had promised Gwendolyn, and I felt I must keep faith with her unless some urgent duty demanded I break it.

Mother got up. "Edith, I don't suppose it will take you long to arrange yourself to leave this place, but I should give the girls at least a few days' preparation. I think we might try for Friday. Would that suit you? Edith?"

I was silent. The thing I had to say would change a lot of things, and I was hesitant.

Father looked at me. "Is something the matter?"

"I'd like to stay on a little," I said. They stared at me in disbelief. "For Gwendolyn. Until she gets things on a better footing here. She oughtn't to be alone. It doesn't seem fair."

"Edith, it's what she herself chose. You saw that," said Father.

"Yes, but I don't think she felt she had a choice, really. But I do have a choice. And I want to help her. It won't be forever, don't worry. I'll be back home and scribbling away again there before you miss me. And the girls can have my room until you get the spare room ready." I'd talked myself into a cheerful frame of mind by now. My parents were both looking at me somewhat quizzically.

There was a tiny furrow of concern between Mother's brows. "You won't…stop writing, will you, Edith?"

"Oh, heavens, no! I've a deadline. But bless you for asking."

Father looked at me thoughtfully. "You like it here."

"I'm not at all sure I do!" I laughed. "But I like Gwendolyn, and I think she needs me—at least for a little. You know I've a pretty good head for business, so I think perhaps I can help."

Mother and Father were taking this sudden change in attitude rather well. I'd never been a great one for making bosom friends, nor would I have been much for sacrificing my own routine for them if they had existed.

I smiled at them. "Mother said something rather unsettling the other day. She said I'd buried my heart in a box. Perhaps now's as a good time as any for digging it up."

Mother patted me on the shoulder. "What a good idea, Edith. Only, do remember, when one takes one's heart out of a box, one must be aware that it may be hurt." I wondered what exactly she was warning me about with those words.

"Well, I'm all for it, so long as none of it involves any caves, Edith," said Father, rather lightly, but I sensed a warning and a plea in his words, on behalf of both of them. "This family needs its young people more than it needs any more hidden treasure."

"I've had quite enough mortal danger for a while, I assure you! I expect Gwendolyn and I will be doing a lot of tiresome book-keeping together instead of having adventures."

But I was wrong, of course.

CHAPTER FOURTEEN

For the next three days the household was busy with the plan to return home. George was sorry to leave a place so rich with possibilities for naturalism (thanks heavens he didn't know just how rich it was in that regard) but Mother and I both felt there was an element of relief also. Though his spirit was as strong and supple as a birch sapling, being callously abandoned in a cave by a man he had trusted must have left a mark on it. We both thought time at home in his normal surroundings would restore him more quickly.

Violet and Una were both elated, in their different ways. Una walked about in a dream, her eyes fastened on Mother like she had in very truth found her guiding angel. Violet was full of questions and plans. The features of an English town were as unknown to her as an Oriental bazaar was to me. She had never ridden a train or visited a sweet shop. I almost regretted not being the one to introduce her to these wonders, especially the latter. I gave her tuppence to spend there in my memory.

Things were not as cheery for Gwendolyn. I'd told her

my plan to stay on a while, but it hadn't relieved her as much as I'd hoped. I suppose my offer of a few weeks or months of companionship wasn't much, when she had committed to give her entire youth to the estate.

Also, Drake had not returned since he'd abruptly left our meeting in the tower that day, and this weighed on her.

"You mustn't think badly of him, Edith," said Gwendolyn, looking tired, as we sat together in the fire in my study on the Friday evening. "If it hadn't been for Simon, I would have gone to pieces after Father and Percy died. He was everything to me then."

I reassured her, but I did think a little badly of him. The man confused me. I had first seen him as a Heathcliff or Rochester, the kind of brooding, masterful man I wanted nothing to do with. Then I had seen him in the wood, and he had appeared quite differently to me, almost as a figure from a fairy-tale. Not, however, as the hero who breaks the spell, but as the cursed prince who is under one, like the dear bear in Grimms.

I understood that I'd shaken him deeply by my words that afternoon. I'd questioned the honour and morality of his actions, and I'd openly excoriated his ancestors. But Gwendolyn hadn't fallen into hysterics and I certainly hadn't expected Drake to do so. I tried to reserve my judgement, but I wasn't entirely successful.

"He's probably taking care of his mother," she said thoughtfully.

"His mother?" I repeated in surprise.

"Yes. His mother. She's an invalid. She's the one who introduced me to Inspector Green. I didn't know books could be like that. She's a great reader."

I reflected with interest on this new image of Drake as possessing a mother who was holed up in bed, forever reading yellow-back novels.

"Anyway, I'm sure he'll be here tomorrow. He has to be." Gwendolyn's tone made me instantly nervous.

"To say goodbye to everyone, you mean?" I said cautiously.

"Well, yes."

"Gwendolyn. What else?"

"It's almost the full moon."

My head spun. "The full moon? What precisely are we expecting at the full moon? Vampires?"

"Don't be silly," she snapped (a little unfairly, I thought). "But the wyvern does come out sometimes when it oughtn't. And usually Simon…"

"The wyvern?" I almost shrieked, recalling the angry winged creature I'd seen depicted at the train station.

"Don't worry, your family will be gone by then—"

"And we'll be alone with the wyvern!" I was losing my head a little.

"No, no, of course we won't be alone! Simon will be here."

"And what will Simon do with the wyvern?" I was now somewhere between laughter and blind panic.

"Stop saying wyvern every sentence, Edith, it's absurd. He'll take care of it for us. You won't have to worry about it at all. I don't know why you offered to stay if you're going to panic every moment," she said severely. This was the old Gwendolyn and it calmed me a bit. She looked at me sideways and pursed her lips. "All the same, I suppose I ought to show you the Muniments Room."

"The Mu—"

"No, don't go repeating everything I'm saying, you'll drive me distracted. I'll show you tomorrow when the household is quiet again. It's where we keep all of our things. The things we don't let outsiders see."

I thought of the antidote she'd assured me about; it must be there. I felt somewhat relieved.

She got up briskly. "I'll go to bed now. I don't want any more questions now."

"Good night, Gwendolyn," I said. She was slipping out the door when she paused.

"Oh, I finished the novel, and you were quite right," she said.

My heart jumped. "Did you like it?"

But she had gone. And I was left wondering what exactly I had been right about.

I was about to get my candle and go to bed when I remembered that I'd put a spare handkerchief in one of the drawers and should send it to be laundered. I pulled open the drawer and saw something very odd: an envelope, marked TO MISS EDITH WORMS.

And then I remembered why I had put my handkerchief in the drawer. I had wrapped Francis's defunct skin in it in case it was dangerous. The handkerchief and the skin were entirely gone, replaced by a mysterious missive addressed to myself.

I picked it up. I had a horrible feeling that I'd seen the handwriting before, but only once. I opened it carefully and read it by the light of my candle.

Miss Worms,

I was prevented from communicating fully to you due to the misguided aggression of the varanus salvator and your own height-ened emotional state. I had planned to reveal to you that I represent a party who, out of the purest scientific and naturalistic motives, has an interest in the unique fauna of your family estate.

You should know that my legal advice to your family has remained confidential and of the highest expertise. The estate is in financial difficulties. The party I represent is eager to provide the most generous financial compensation in return for the privilege of exclusive access to the fauna of the estate. I hope I do not need to explain what advantages might come to you personally from this. When you wish to communicate with this party, who desires to remain anonymous, please do so through me, at the following address.

Cordially at your service,

John Rivers

I SAT DOWN. For a moment I was back in the cave in utter darkness, gripping a dead man's arm, and finding the bandage that covered the wound that had killed him.

When I had questioned George about it later, he told me that Rivers had grown increasingly bad-tempered during their exploration of the cave, and had complained of a pain in his arm, murmuring something about an infection and an idiot girl.

Now the man had posthumously revealed a further facet to the mystery. He had been hired by person or persons unknown to poke around the Abbey and the estate for evidence of…what precisely? Dragons, certainly, but had he understood that? Had his employer? Rivers had shown me that Francis had mythic properties but how fully had he grasped the import of them? He had called Francis a varanid lizard, never a salamander. But he must have understood something was special about Francis since he had stolen my handkerchief along with a piece of evidence. Ought I to search his effects for it?

I dismissed these lesser questions. I must show Gwendolyn the letter. And I knew it would deeply unsettle her. I folded it back up and put it in my pocket.

I took my candle and began to make the journey to my room, searching my heart to find pity for him. I found little there. He had died because he refused to ask for help and because he was intent upon some villainy which was still opaque to me. I prayed that he had no dependants. Father had written to his firm. Drake, as the local magistrate, had informed the authorities and done everything necessary. Father told me he had gone down to the cave entrance with Drake and there read the Order for the Burial of the Dead from the Prayer Book.

For man walketh in a vain shadow, and disquieteth himself in vain: he heapeth up riches, and cannot tell who shall gather them. How very apt.

I had come by now to the Great Staircase and I felt a chill as I remembered my encounter with the man there. I shook myself and was about to continue when it occurred to me that it might be worth taking a look behind the tapestry right now, when I could reproduce more closely the conditions under which Rivers had looked at it.

I found that for some reason, I very much did not want to do that. The darkness in the Great Hall was dense, my light was small, and there was a feeling of a spaciousness about me that was full of unpleasant possibilities. It was no mere fancy to think that anything might be lurking there, watching me, as I myself had watched Rivers that night.

I turned on my heel and took my unwilling self over to the tapestries. Without thinking too hard, I made my hand reach out where I thought his might have been that night. I pushed aside the tapestry and allowed the light of my candle to fall behind it.

I felt my heart stop for an instant. It was the picture of the children being thrown to the monsters.

The smaller scale of these figures made them perceivable at this distance. Their faces were contorted in terror. A horned, scaled creature with two clawed feet and wings gaped wide its mouth to receive them. And I knew why Rivers had taken George, a child, into those caves.

George had been taken as an offering.

I felt sick for a moment. The letter in my pocket was so hateful to me that I almost burnt it then and there. Had he already planned to kill my brother when he wrote it?

Rivers must have taken George as a kind of insurance. He gambled that if there was any truth to the myth of dragons guarding the treasure, he might placate or distract them by throwing my brother to them. I thought of my Father, dutifully saying the burial prayers at the cave for the man who'd intended to kill his only son.

A bit shakily, I made my way up the stairs and to my room. I was too sick and angry to show Gwendolyn the letter tonight. It wasn't until I was lying in bed that I remembered the monster in the fresco.

Wings and horns, sharp curving claws. A long, jagged tongue poking out. A barbed tail and feathered wings. Two legs instead of four. A belly that almost scraped the ground.

It was a wyvern.

CHAPTER FIFTEEN

The next day brought torrential rain, making travel impossible, perhaps even for a couple of days.

Everyone had been ready for the trip and it was one of those days when children are likely to do naughty things. Regardless, I was not sorry to delay being left in an empty gothic Abbey to battle mythical beasts with Gwendolyn, though she seemed very tetchy about it.

Thankfully, Mother took charge of the situation. She took the girls to the sitting room and in no time had them making paper dolls and dresses for them out of the scrap-bag while she read Grimms to them. George was given a Henty book she'd been keeping for such a time as this. I went and sat with them for a while, just to be near them.

The bright fire and the girls' faces as they listened cheered me. George was lying on the rug next to Francis, reading his book in a state of deep concentration. It did me good to sit there and just watch him breathe. He was alive, and it was Rivers who had been left in the cave to be devoured by monsters.

And though after my skin worms destroy this body; yet in my flesh shall I see God: whom I shall see for myself, and mine eyes shall behold, and not another. But unlike Job, I did not think Rivers would be glad to see Him when the time came.

Gwendolyn was standing in the doorway. She raised an eyebrow at me and then went away. I could tell she wanted me to follow. I sighed and went after her. I knew how to be insistent and get my way most of the time when I really wanted it, but to command another with a raised eyebrow? This was beyond my powers.

"Where are we going?" I asked as I followed her.

"I told you, the Muniments Room," she answered shortly.

"But this is my tower," I said.

"It's not your tower, it's William's Tower." She opened a door with her set of keys and we went up a stair that led to the bit of the roof that butted into the tower.

"Who's William?" I asked, but I was silenced by driving rain. We made a short dash in the elements to another door, which I saw at once would let us into the room immediately above mine.

I don't know what I expected. Though I consider myself a reasonably imaginative person, I simply didn't have a picture in my head for Forbidden Room of Ancient Dragon Secrets.

The octagonal room appeared smaller than my own because it was completely crowded with objects. There were bunches of herbs hanging from the ceiling; shelves of jars with murky contents, vials, and pottery ointment jars; a shelf of scrolls and fat notebooks with papers spilling out.

Hanging on one wall was what appeared to be a farrier's tools: large shears, pincers, and clippers. My eyes followed those to a selection of muzzles of varying sizes—some alarmingly large. Nearby were harnesses, coils of rope…was that some kind of *saddle* mounted on the wall?

There was a glass case with a naturalist's collection of eggs, feathers, iridescent scales, and a tiny upright skeleton that resembled a chicken with a very long tailbone, all carefully marked with labels in flowing copperplate. There was an octagonal marble table in the centre of the room that was kept clear and I could see that people had scratched their names into it for centuries.

I could tell Gwendolyn was nervous at bringing me here and she was making up for it by acting like everything was completely normal. Now she was moving some crates around as if she was looking for something.

"Gwendolyn," I whispered.

"You don't need to whisper," she said, sensibly enough.

"Where are the weapons?" I asked, in what I hoped was a normal tone.

"What do you mean?"

"For the wyvern. You know."

"No. I don't know," she retorted, pulling out a box. "Ah!" She set the box down in front of us on the table. It was labelled simply but effectively: WYVERN. I was eager to see what dread weapon it might contain to defeat such a beast.

She opened the lid. Inside was what appeared to me to be an elegantly carved musical instrument. She looked pleased.

"Are we going to play the flute to it?" I asked at last.

Gwendolyn turned her head and froze me with her expression.

"It's a blow gun, Edith. Darts come out of it."

"Oh. Well, what about another sort of gun? As an extra precaution?"

Her look did not thaw even one degree.

"Perhaps a Winchester? I hear those are quite effective," I suggested.

Both eyebrows went up. "You don't mean those things that American cowboys use?" she said this as if I'd suggested the most outlandish of mythical weapons (Excalibur, perhaps).

"You don't mean you are going to try to kill the creature with a blow-gun?" I asked, a little impatiently.

"Kill it? Why would we kill it?"

"Well, what *do* we do with it?"

"We have to put it in a holding cell."

"Until it's time to kill it?"

"No!" She took a step back from me. "We're *wardens*, Edith, not dragon slayers. Wait—" She looked at me, eyes widening. "All this time, did you think we were dragon slayers? Is that what you thought?"

"I don't know!" I burst out. "They're always killing them in stories. What else does one *do* with dragons?"

Gwendolyn laughed, and kept on laughing. It stopped me completely because it was the first time I'd ever heard it. It was a very nice sound; throatier and less aristocratic than I would have imagined. She sat down on a crate and sighed.

"Well, I suppose it's all ridiculous, isn't it?"

"Just a little," I admitted.

She was quiet for a moment. "Haven't you thought of the name?"

"You mean, Worms? Well, yes, of course. I've always known it was the old word for dragon. It comes from the Anglo-Saxon, 'wyrm' with a 'y'."

"I mean the name of the Abbey."

"The herb? Wormwood? Artemisia, isn't it?"

"But that's not what it is at all. Our family have been Worm Wardens since Christianity came to the Dale. So you see, it's not Worm-wood," she continued patiently. "It's—"

"Worm Ward," I finished. We looked at each other.

"We're Worm Wardens, Edith. I suppose one might say 'Dragon Keepers' today."

I sat on the crate next to her.

"And you say you haven't an education."

"Oh, all this?" She gestured about the room dismissively. "It's not the real world, is it?"

"Isn't it?" I asked. I looked around me at the array of tools and objects. "It seems very real to me."

"Thank you," she said quietly. "For being here with me."

Her mood instantly changed to business-like, she sprang up and started gathering items into a basket.

"We'll have to keep watch tonight. Rest if you can, during the day. We begin our watch at moonrise."

MOONRISE FOUND the two of us on top of William's Tower. For the first time since I'd met her, neither of us were in mourning. I had dressed for warmth and freedom of movement. Gwendolyn was swathed in her father's great coat. She was a tall woman, so she looked impressive rather than ridiculous. Though she had scoffed at my mention of vampires, tonight I thought that I'd rather go hunting monsters with Gwendolyn than anyone else in the world.

She had brought a lantern, but hadn't kindled it yet. The moonlight was enough, and we'd see the surrounding countryside better this way.

The night was clear with the kind of diamond-clarity I had seen from my window a month ago, and from here the Abbey was laid out around us so that we could see most of it very well. Only the ruin was an impenetrable mass of shadows.

Gwendolyn had informed me that the wyvern's regular place of hibernation was very near the Abbey and if it came out tonight, this would give us the best vantage point from which to spot it.

"Simon will be here soon," she announced, but I didn't think she sounded sure. I thought of ivy and stone walls again. It always irritated me to see how much Gwendolyn relied on Drake. This time I let the irritation drive me to ask the question I'd so badly wanted an answer to since my second day at the Abbey.

"Gwendolyn, why did you want me to fall in love with him?"

There might have been a better way to ask this question, but I don't know what it was. One doesn't beat about the bush when one is standing on a tower at moonrise watching for a wyvern.

She stared at me, but I couldn't entirely read her expression in the moonlight.

"How did you…?"

"I overheard, unintentionally."

"Oh."

She still hadn't answered my question.

"Is it because you wanted me to stay?"

There was an owl hooting, down in the wood. It called twice before she answered.

"Yes."

"You must have been very desperate, to give up the man you love."

I heard a sharp intake of breath. I wondered if my comment had struck too deeply, but I wanted her to know that she had nothing to fear from me as a rival.

"Is that what you—oh, Edith. It was wrong of me to try to keep you here that way. But you should know, I'm not in love with Simon."

"But—"

"Oh, I was once. When I was eleven or so. But I couldn't keep it going. It was always assumed we would marry whether we loved each other or not, and I suppose that killed it, if nothing else. There's nothing quite like being raised with someone and told they are going to be your future spouse day in and day out to make that kind of feeling quite impossible. But I suppose I would have just fallen in with it anyway." There was a defeated tone to her voice.

"What happened?"

"Simon. He said no. About a year ago, when they started talking about publishing the banns. There was the most awful row. I don't think Father ever really accepted it. He was Simon's godfather, you know, and ever since Simon's own father died he got harder and harder on him."

I had never thought so well of Drake as I did now.

"I made such a fool of myself after Father died. I felt so alone. I told Simon that I was in love with him. But it was a dreadful lie, and he knew it. He always knew me better than my own father and brother did."

"But why?"

She leaned on the parapet, looking out over the Abbey. The clouds were clearing now and we could see where they cast shadows out on the fells.

"I don't know quite how to say it. There have always been Worms here. This is what we do. And if we don't, who will? And I was so terribly afraid of doing it alone."

"But does it need to be done, Gwendolyn?" I said this in the gentlest tone possible.

The owl called again in the silence.

"I don't know." Her voice was very small. This was the vulnerable Gwendolyn again, the one that made me think of a child that was paralysed with fear of doing the wrong thing. "I know nothing of the world outside this place. If we don't take care of them, if they come out at lambing season and decimate the flocks…if they wander and spread beyond the Dale, what will happen?" She looked at me.

"I—I don't know." But I did know, at least a bit. There must be some way to profit from the beasts and that would attract the worst sorts of people. I had met one dragon hunter already in the person of Rivers. If he was any indication at all, the future of the people and animals of Wormwood Abbey at the hands of such men was a very unpleasant one.

"That's why I admire your mother," she said, startling me. "She had a courage I don't. She left everything."

I rapidly sorted through my thoughts as I spoke. "My mother left everything because she believed there was something more important, something worth losing everything for. You have courage, Gwendolyn. It's just— you ought to be sure that it's worth the cost to stay here. Even Christ says we should count the cost before we begin."

"The cost? You mean the cost of my life? How many people have given their lives to this, Edith? Why should mine be any different? What's special about me?"

"Their choices are not yours, Gwendolyn!" She was overwrought and I was pushing her too hard, but I couldn't bear her hopelessness.

"But they are!" Her voice was rising now. "Don't you see? I haven't the courage to be the one who makes it all mean nothing. All of the lives, all of the deaths, all of the sacrifices and the buried hopes. Don't you see? Whoever is the one to finally throw the whole thing over, they'll be the villain of the story. They'll be the curse that fell. They'll be the fall of the house of Worms. And I simply don't have what it takes to do it! I'm a coward."

I felt completely helpless in the face of this. Was that really what this place was? I thought of the ancient peoples of the Dale, throwing their children to the dragons. Oh, yes, we had Christianised it, certainly, but it was still a place of human sacrifice. Only now, instead of throwing our children to the dragons, we buried them alive here.

She had covered her face with her hands. I put my hand on her shoulder. I thought of how I'd promised to help her bear her burden. Of how she'd warned me that her friendship might be costly. My heart was wrung for her, but what could I do? What part could I play in this? What part was I able to play?

I knew one thing: hers was a part I could not play. I had no training or inclination for this role, and if it was wrong for her to bury herself alive here, it would be wrong also for me. As these thoughts were going through my mind, I stared down at the walk at the side of the house. There was a bush there I didn't remember, casting a strange shadow. A shadow with a tail. My heart jolted.

"Gwendolyn," I whispered. "Is that…."

She looked up. She was instantly serious. "Yes. We need to get to it before it leaves the open ground. It will be much harder if it gets into the Abbey. And if it gets onto the fells it will be in amongst the lambs in no time."

And with those words, my cousin and I were off to hunt a dragon.

CHAPTER SIXTEEN

When we got to the ground floor, we regrouped in the kitchen. I saw that under the greatcoat, Gwendolyn had a wide belt around her waist with objects attached: the blowpipe and a pouch, a vial of some kind (the promised antidote, no doubt), and a stout coil of rope.

My fingers were itching for a weapon of some sort. I would have given my kingdom for a Winchester, whatever Gwendolyn said about Americans.

"Don't I get a dragon-hunting kit? I feel a little bare."

She gave me an appraising look, then grabbed a large knife in a plain leather sheath from a kitchen shelf and handed it to me. "You're not clumsy are you? You won't hurt yourself?"

"Gwendolyn, this is a kitchen knife," I objected.

"That's what you think. Actually it's a dragon hunting knife that's been in the family since King Henry."

"Which King Henry?" I looked at the knife with interest.

"Would you mind saving historical questions for later?

Now, remember what I told you: if we can keep it on open ground I can get it within range of my blow pipe. Once it's drugged, it will be much easier to take it to the holding cell below the Abbey."

She was moving again, taking the unlit lantern with her. I followed her closely.

"What happens to it after that?"

"We keep it there until summer, when the lambs are grown. The shepherds move their flocks further upland when it's dragon season."

Now we were outside, around the corner from where I'd seen the creature below us, I thought. Gwendolyn had given me various instructions for interacting with it. Apparently, they were very seldom disposed to attack humans, preferring prey smaller than themselves and preferably incapacitated. They sometimes ate their prey entire. Gwendolyn assured me that I was too big for this kind of treatment. I had never wished so fervently that I was tall. Gwendolyn said if I was really worried about it I should raise my arms above my head to increase my stature. She also suggested I strenuously object if it began to bite me, but I hadn't thought those instructions necessary at all and had told her so.

"You've got the antidote here, haven't you?" I whispered.

"Yes, I've got it with me, now hush."

We rounded the corner quietly. The shadow was gone.

"Blast!" she hissed.

We heard a scatter of claws from within the ruined Abbey church and looked at each other. It was inside.

"Oh, no," she said. "That makes things a bit more complicated."

"Couldn't we just wait outside for it to come out?"

"There are too many ways it could get out. It would be gone and we wouldn't know."

"Do you mean…we'll have to go in?"

She struck a light and lit the lantern. Her face looked grim in the lantern light, the lines weirdly emphasised by the shadows it cast. "We should stay together."

No fear of me running off, I thought.

Quietly, we approached the ruins. The gap in the wall was a black void like the entrance to the cave had been.

We sidled in. I stayed very close to her and gripped the knife sheath hard. At first I'd been glad of the light but now I wished we'd gone in without it. The lantern swung about as we moved, despite her obvious efforts to keep it steady, making the blackness jump around us like an angry cat. I had to be careful not to trip on bits of fallen masonry.

The worst part was approaching each alcove in the walls. At first, each one was inky black and then a figure would appear to leap out of it at us. Of course they were all saints battling monsters, with snouts and bared teeth protruding horribly. And worst of all was the expectation that in one of those alcoves a real monster would be waiting. I began to resent those medieval stonemasons.

Suddenly there was a scrabbling sound in the dark in front of us. Now Gwendolyn was off in hot pursuit, streaking away in a leaping circle of light. She disappeared out the main entrance of the church and I was left in the dark. Of course I should have stuck with her, but in the moment when she moved away the blackness took me. I was paralysed with a sudden fear that left me breathless. I felt once again the cold damp air and the pressure of the earth over my head, as of a great weight.

I looked up and saw the rose window with stars in it. They were not glow worms, but real stars, with familiar constellations. I breathed again. I was not in an underground cave. I was in the ruin of the Abbey Church, the monster had fled, and my cousin needed my help.

I could see a little better now so I started to move as quickly as I dared, reluctant to risk turning my ankle on the uneven ground. Suddenly I fell over something. I let out a cry, because the object I fell over was all too familiar to me. I had come across something in the dark like it before. It was a man's body. Fear and horror surged through me. I caught myself with one hand on the ground.

"Gwen?" a voice said quietly.

I nearly yelled again in relief. Thank God, this one wasn't dead. A wave of guilt I'd never let myself feel for Rivers flooded over me and I was instantly in tears.

"Miss Worms?" The voice sounded faintly horrified.

"Mr Drake," I replied, trying to sound more sane than I presently was. "Are you hurt?"

"Bitten, on the leg," he answered with remarkable coolness. "I'm not certain if it envenomated me. But it's not safe for me to walk. It circulates the venom."

As my eyes adjusted I could make out his face a bit in the moonlight from one of the windows. He was lying on the ground, propping himself up on one elbow.

"Gwendolyn has the antidote, I'll go after her and bring her back at once, I know time is of the essence."

Was I imagining things or did he stare at me quite intensely?

"Miss Worms?"

I was already stumbling off in my haste. I turned back for an instant.

"Yes?"

"I apologise for upsetting you."

"No, Mr. Drake," I corrected him, remembering the

last time we had met, when I had questioned his honour. "It is I who should apologise for upsetting you."

I wouldn't stay for any more chit-chat. It may have been somewhat my fault that Rivers had been fatally bitten. Francis was protecting me, after all. But I was determined that this bite would not go untreated a minute longer than I could help. I would have no part in another man's death.

Once I'd gotten out of the church, the realisation hit me that I had no idea which way Gwendolyn had gone. I had no Pilot to guide me this time. She might be chasing the beast across the fells, or any direction round the buildings. For a moment I was frozen with indecision.

It was then that I heard a sound from the direction of the cloisters. I quickly ran there. As I entered the cloisters, I slowed down. I looked around the four sides, wondering if the creature was even now hiding in one of the dark corners which my eyes could not penetrate. I could see no sign of Gwendolyn's lantern. Had I chosen the wrong direction?

The moonlight illuminated the herb garden brightly, so my eye was drawn there. Everything seemed normal and peaceful there, from the moon-white clusters of narcissus to the statue in the middle of the garden. I was turning to leave when I remembered: there was no statue in the middle of the garden. I had seen Mother and Una there only the other day, and thought there should be one. A figure of a saint, I'd thought.

But this was no saint. It was a monster.

I moved a step closer to the garden. It did not move at all. Was it really a statue? Had it been there all along? I was now standing half in moonlight and half in shadow, where the cloister roof ended and the garden began.

The figure in the garden was utterly still. It was about

the size of Pilot and had upright ears similar to a different breed of dog. But there the resemblance ended. It balanced on two legs like a bird of prey, with talons like a hawk and spurs like a cockerel. Its low belly and back were scaled, but its folded wings were feathered, though with what colours I could only imagine. Its tail curled behind it before ending in a kind of barb. I was motionless, lost in awe at this creature of legend before me.

Suddenly, its tongue flickered out, the first movement I'd seen from it. Was it putting out its tongue to get my scent, to determine whether I was a threat to it? The tongue reminded me of Francis.

Standing before this creature, I felt no fear at all, only a kind of cautious respect, a reverence even. This was no monster!

I recalled Mother's words to Una in this very place.

All of God's creatures are beautiful and useful, though not all of them are pleasant.

There was a movement in the cloisters to my right. It was Gwendolyn, lifting something to her mouth, her eyes fixed on the wyvern. Then I heard the sound of something moving through the air and the wyvern startled. Its wings flung out and gave two or three powerful flaps. The creature began rising up, and my heart lifted with its flight for an instant; I felt a rush of air on my face.

All of a sudden, it faltered and dropped to the ground, emitting a sad, strange, birdlike sound. And then it seemed to lose consciousness, crumpling on its side.

My fears for Drake rushed back to me.

"Gwendolyn!" I called, running towards her. "It's Drake."

She had been uncoiling her rope but she stopped instantly.

"He's hurt," I finished.

"You left him?" She sounded horrified.

"To find you!"

"Quickly, show me."

We ran back to the ruin together and felt our way back to him. She dropped down by his side.

"Simon! What have you done? Don't move!"

"I'm sorry, Gwen. I'd almost gotten a rope round it when I tripped on a loose stone. I've made a mess of things."

"It's all right, we got it ourselves." As she spoke she'd been relighting her lamp. In the light of it I saw Drake turn his head to look at me in surprise.

"Edith did a marvellous job. She distracted it for me."

I did? Well, yes, I suppose I did.

"Gwen, hadn't we better give him the antidote?" I begged. "You can both praise me as much as you like after that."

They looked at each other. And then at me.

"What? You do have the antidote, don't you? You promised me you had it."

"I said it was with me. It is. But I don't have it. You have it."

I was aghast.

"Gwendolyn, how can you say so? You know I don't!"

"But you do."

"Stop it!" I was getting angry—confused and angry.

"Edith. You are the antidote."

That pulled me up short. "What do you mean?"

"The antidote is you."

I shook my head to clear it. The world was spinning. "What are you saying?"

Drake nodded at Gwendolyn. She swallowed and spoke in a very steady tone.

"Edith, you're a special kind of person. Simon and I both knew it when we met. It's your hair."

"My hair!"

"I told you, it pops up in our family now and then, and it's very prized. Your kind of person always has it."

"But how can my hair—"

"No, the hair just shows us what you are. It's a clue. And the way you took to Francis is another one. You're a *Marsi*, Edith. You can heal dragon bites, and you're immune to their poisons."

If it hadn't been for the last part of her sentence, I think I would have left then and there. But it explained exactly what had happened to me with Francis, which was a question I had set aside in all the excitement of the last few days, and it had the ring of truth.

"Why didn't you tell me this before?"

Gwendolyn looked down.

"I'm so sorry, Edith, I—"

Drake answered. "I asked her not to."

"But why?"

Was it my imagination or did he flush in the lamplight? Gwendolyn answered for him.

"Simon didn't want you to…to feel like you had to stay here with us. To feel you had no choice."

It took me half a second, but then I understood. In a family which kept poisonous beasts, an antidote was priceless. And somehow, in a way I didn't yet understand, that antidote was me. *I* was priceless. Drake believed that I had the kind of conscience that would not allow me to abandon them when their need was so serious. And he had refused to use that to constrain my free choice.

I got down on my knees next to them. "What do I do?" I asked in a low voice.

Gwendolyn showed me the bite near Drake's ankle. It

appeared as two discreet puncture wounds. Nothing like the gory horror I'd imagined.

"You have to spit on it."

"Spit on it?"

"Yes."

I stared at her. Her lips were compressed with stress.

"Are you sure?" I balked.

"Yes, I'm sure. And would you mind doing it sometime soon?"

"Are—are you sure I don't have to suck out the poison?"

"What a disgusting idea. Just please spit on it. Right there."

My mouth had never felt more dry. I felt suddenly convinced that I would never be able to spit again. How did one spit? I'd seen my brother and his playmates spit; great gobs of it. How did they do it? Why didn't they teach girls *useful* things?

"Edith, please."

I was feeling a little light-headed.

"What if I can't do it?"

"Look at me, Edith. Do you still have the knife? The knife I gave you?"

"Uh, yes—yes, I do." I found I was still gripping it.

"All right, then. If you can't spit on it, we'll have to cut off his foot. Ready?"

I was in such an altered mental state right now that cutting off his foot sounded about as difficult as spitting on it. But it was picturing Drake without both a thumb and a foot that cleared my head.

This man had not tried to keep me here, he had not tried to make me fall in love with him. He had treated me fairly, very fairly indeed, when he might have tried all sorts of persuasions against me in his interests. He had asked nothing of me.

I remembered how I had seen him in the wood, looking like a prince under a curse. This was it. He was the prince who slept in the enchanted wood under a spell, and I was the one sent to break it. I must not fail.

I spat, quite a lot. Gwendolyn told me it was enough. She had a handkerchief in her hand and rubbed it into the puncture wounds briskly. I wiped my mouth with the back of my hand, manners forgotten.

Then she said, "You might try giving him a kiss as well," very casually, just as if she'd read my mind about the fairy tale.

"Will that help?" I asked seriously.

"It can't hurt," she answered cheerily. I stared at her. I think that was the first time she'd ever joked with me. I wasn't sure which shocked me more, her suggestion that I kiss this recumbent young man or the fact that she had told a joke.

At this, Drake, who'd been amazingly quiet all this time, remonstrated with her.

"Gwen! For goodness' sake." But there was laughter as well as indignation in his voice.

Having done my duty, I sat back on my heels.

"What now?"

"We have to strap the wyvern onto a pallet and take it down to its cell."

"Hadn't we better strap Mr. Drake there instead?"

"What do you say, Simon, would you like to be tied onto the pallet?" queried Gwendolyn, with a spark of humour in her voice. She was in very good spirits.

Drake laughed.

"I appreciate Miss Worms' concern, but no. I'll just lie here for ten minutes and then join you."

"But what if—what if I'm not the thing you said?"

"A Marsi?" asked Gwendolyn.

"Yes." But even as I said it, I knew I was. Francis's scales should have killed me and they didn't. I was immune to dragon poisons, just as Gwendolyn said. She was looking into my eyes and I think she saw my thought somehow.

"You are." She said this with complete faith. There was a longing on her face as she said it. I'd seen it once or twice before and now I understood it. I'd even seen it on Drake's face, the day we met. It was the way one looks at a view of the hills when one has been cooped up inside for too long, or at a warm fire through a neighbour's window when one is frozen and stiff from tramping through the snow.

It had puzzled me before but it puzzled me no longer. Now, it sent a shiver of mingled elation and fear through me.

I had a power I had never dreamt of, but what did it mean? For me, and for them?

The next quarter of an hour were taken up by manoeuvring the sleeping wyvern onto a pallet with wheels. I thought I would shudder to touch the creature, but I found its scales just as pleasant as I found Francis's, and its feathers were soft as silk.

Drake joined us partway into this process. His hair was awry and his collar undone. But there was a smile on his face and I thought he'd never looked more friendly. He wanted to pull the pallet along for us but Gwendolyn and I insisted on doing it so he could mind his ankle as he walked.

We were bringing the creature into the kitchen yard, and whispering and laughing together. I felt a little elated after surviving the events of the evening and I had invented a ridiculous elocution lesson to mock the ones that Gwendolyn told me her old governesses had drilled into them. Mine was all about dragging drugged dragons and it had made them both laugh, which made me feel ridiculously happy. It reminded me of the feeling of satisfaction I got when I was near the end of writing one of my novels, except this was a moment shared with two people I found I very much liked.

Pilot burst out of the scullery at that moment and bounded up to Drake in palpable relief. There was a kerfuffle and a cluster of people spilled out of the scullery after him, clearly roused from sleep by the anxious Pilot.

Gwendolyn and I stopped dragging the thing and the three of us stood stock still, like children caught raiding the larder. None of us was stout enough to obstruct a fully grown wyvern from the surprised view of my parents, George, Violet, and Una, who were now standing before us in their nightclothes and dressing gowns, looking understandably disturbed.

Father was fumbling to put on his glasses, as if that would make the wyvern any more comprehensible. Mother had frozen with her hand on Father's arm. Violet was elbowing George in excitement and Una was holding on to the back of Mother's dressing gown.

I felt this was the time to say something important but I couldn't think of a thing that would make the situation any easier. Then it came to me.

"You were quite right, Father. You did see a dragon in the garden. We found it."

CHAPTER SEVENTEEN

Twenty minutes later we were all seated around the kitchen table with cups of strong tea. I think Father had a bit of brandy also. Gwendolyn and Simon had disappeared with the wyvern to parts unknown (refusing George's excited offer to assist them), and I had given my parents a brief sketch of the evening's events. Then they came back and joined us. Gwendolyn apologised to Father for not confiding in him, and as usual he was very graceful about it.

"So you see, Father, it's not Wormwood like the plant —" I began, thinking to impress him with my linguistic prowess.

"Oh, of course, Edith, it's Worm-Ward, that much was obvious," he said a little impatiently. "And Ormdale— that's Old Norse for Valley of the Dragon. Anyone can see that."

I felt a bit quenched.

"But my dear," said Mother to me, wonderingly. "Did you already know all this the other day when you decided to stay on with Gwendolyn?"

"Yes! Well, most of it. At least, I didn't know I was a magical person until about midnight."

Gwendolyn made a slight sound. "It's not magic, Edith."

"All right. I suppose it's like this: some people get terribly sick if a bee or a wasp stings them, and some don't. Dragons make all of you sick, but they're just fine for me," I said. Possibly I was a touch smug.

"Do you think I've got it, too?" asked George hopefully.

Mother, Father, Gwendolyn, Drake, and I all said *NO* very firmly to this at the same time. George was quelled for the moment.

"I'm not sure that quite works, dear," said Mother. "After all, people who don't get sick with insect stings can't spit on people who do to make them better."

This was a reasonable point.

"What's more, I don't suppose this…well, this 'magic' that Edith seems to have stops her from getting hurt by a dragon that really wants to hurt her, does it?" Mother looked at Gwendolyn and Simon questioningly. "It wouldn't stop one eating her, would it?"

They looked at each other.

Gwendolyn's lips compressed again. "Aunt Emily, I'm not sure this will relieve your feelings, but dragons don't, as a rule, eat people. People generally kick up too much of a fuss. Infants, of course, should be strictly watched, but there aren't any in the family at present. Dragons keep to themselves unless they need food, and then they prefer small animals like lambs and rabbits who don't fight back. I can assure you after a month in her company, your daughter is no rabbit."

This made me glow inwardly.

Father looked at Simon. "Didn't one bite Drake just now?"

"It was entirely my fault, sir," Simon answered. "I provoked it. I was attempting to restrain it."

"Exactly! You did provoke it," I cried. "I'm quite sure if you came at me in the dark with a rope I'd bite you myself."

"Miss Worms, I can assure you I wouldn't even consider it," he said very gravely.

Mother looked between us, her brow slightly furrowed. "Edith, you sound as if you are on the dragons' side."

"Perhaps I am. After all, I'm a Worms, aren't I?"

Everyone went quiet. In the excitement of the moment I had perhaps committed myself a little further than I had intended.

Father pushed back his chair. "Well, now that the creature has been safely contained, I suggest we all go back to bed and get an hour or two of sleep. The children will be the better for it and so will I."

This highly sensible suggestion we all followed directly.

The next day was Sunday but the roads were too wet for us to go to the village church, so Father read Morning Prayer in the Great Hall. I say 'read' because he had his Prayer Book in his hand, but Father knew it all by heart. At home we had Morning Prayer every day except Sunday, when Father was occupied with Divine Service. Father had chosen a reading from the Psalms.

"Praise the Lord from the earth, ye dragons, and all deeps:

Fire, and hail; snow, and vapours; stormy wind fulfilling his word:

Mountains, and all hills; fruitful trees, and all cedars:

Beasts, and all cattle; creeping things, and flying fowl:

Kings of the earth, and all people; princes, and all judges of the earth:

Both young men, and maidens; old men, and children:

Let them praise the name of the Lord: for his name alone is excellent; his glory is above the earth and heaven."

After it was done, he said to me, "Edith, your mother and I would like to talk with you in the sitting room. Gwendolyn, George is much impressed by your knowledge of dragons and would very much like to ask you some scientific questions."

Gwendolyn took George right away. "Come George, I'll show you the Muniments room."

Violet objected. "Gwen, that's not fair, you've never let us in there!"

"All right, you two come as well," said Gwendolyn and led them away.

I followed my parents into the sitting room. The mood was rather sombre.

"Well, Edith, this changes things," began Father, after we'd sat down together.

"Does it?" I asked. "Surely you can see more than ever that Gwendolyn needs me. Please don't make me go home before I've been able to do what I promised and set up the estate better. Surely you can see it's the best thing for everyone."

My parents looked at each other and then back at me.

"Edith, we've no intention of making you do anything. We simply want to understand," explained Mother.

Father looked at me very closely. "Is staying here… what I want to know is, can this be what you really want, Edith?"

This was an excellent question, and I had to reflect on it before I answered. Home was safe, comfortable, and familiar. I knew the Edith who lived and worked there very well. She did not surprise me. The Wormwood Abbey Edith was something quite new.

Last night had been full of terrors but it had also had its joys. The comradeship I'd enjoyed with Gwendolyn, and even with Simon, had been new and delightful to me. And beyond my own feelings and desires there was a growing conviction deep within me that I had a purpose here.

I spoke slowly, weighing my words. "When my mother left her family and her mode of life, was it what she wanted, or what she chose? It may not be what I *want* exactly, but I freely choose it."

Father looked away. Had I hurt him? Mother sighed deeply. "Well. I remember the last time I had a conversation with you like this, and it seems to have gone very much the same way."

"You do? We did?"

I wondered what conversation could possibly compare to one in which I adopted the position of ancestral Dragon Keeper.

Mother laughed. "The one where you told me you wanted to write detective stories."

"And you thought I was ridiculous? You never let on."

"No. I thought—and I still think—that it's a surprising choice for the daughter of a clergyman, and that you might have chosen something easier. But I know now that you are more than equal to counting the cost of an endeavour for yourself, and paying it. What's more, you seem to be able to make it pay *you*, which never ceases to amaze me."

Father was smiling now.

"It seems clear that my ancestors have never been able to make dragon-keeping pay at all. But I feel sure that if anyone can do it, it will certainly be Edith."

. . .

HAVING OBTAINED THIS FILIAL BLESSING, I took advantage of a brief cessation of rain to go on a walk with Francis. George and Violet had bounded up to me with a fine tooled leather collar and lead which they had found in the Muniments Room. It did not fit him yet, but at the rate he was growing I expected it would soon enough. I remembered that some great-grandmother of mine had toured the estate with a feathered bonnet and a capuchin monkey and I felt that with my pet dragon I was well on my way to cutting at least a comparable dash.

After that, I sought out Gwendolyn. I found her putting away some linens in her room.

I'd never been in her bedroom before. It was spartan and meticulous, the room of a woman who had no time for either ornament or disorder. The only bright thing in the room was a set of yellow-back novels on a shelf, exactly corresponding to the number of published Inspector Green books.

"Gwendolyn," I said. "It's all right. They've given me their blessing to stay."

Once again, I was a little disappointed by her reaction.

"Yes," she said simply. "Aunt Emily told me."

"I can't promise to stay for ever, of course."

"No."

"But…it will make things better for you? Won't it? You won't be alone." I found myself feeling dreadfully self-conscious.

"Thank you, Edith. You are very kind. I think I must be the most selfish person in the world."

This startled me.

"Gwendolyn, what do you mean?

"I mean that what you are doing for me is quite marvellous and I should be happy. I really should."

"But?"

She sat quite still, looking down at the linens she had been putting in a drawer a moment ago.

"When I was a child, I was told about Florence Nightingale. One of our governesses had her book, you understand, *Notes on Nursing*. She had so many troubles, people underestimated her, but she had such courage and she was able to do such wonderful things that no one had thought could be done. And then there was the epidemic in '89, and it was so dreadful with the closest doctor as far away as Embsay, and he was old and got sick himself. I've never stopped thinking about it."

I felt like I'd received an electric shock. I had been convinced that Gwendolyn could not imagine a life for herself outside the Dale. But she had. Why had I never simply asked her?

"You want to be a nurse," I said. I felt a bit like crying, but I kept talking to keep my emotions at bay. "I think you'd be simply marvellous. I saw how you were with Simon. And you have a natural authority. They'd put you in charge of a ward in no time."

"No." She looked at me, and I could see a touch of fear in her eyes. "I want to be a doctor."

Well, this completely took my breath away. I sat down.

"Ah," I said. I couldn't think of anything else to say at first. Then I remembered Mother, who hadn't made me feel ridiculous when I came to her at eighteen with the idea of writing detective novels. "Well, there's a medical school for women, isn't there? In London?"

"London!" She said the word as if it was as exotic as Timbuktu.

"Yes, London. The city. It really exists, you know. I've

been there myself. The harder part is…well…you'd need some Latin. But Father could help with that. I was never very keen on it. I'm sure he'd love a more conscientious pupil."

Gwendolyn looked confused. "Edith, what are you talking about? I can't—I can't go to London! I was just telling you about it, just to tell you. Grumbling, really. I suppose everyone has childhood dreams of greatness, but that—"

I stopped her. "Gwen. You have a first-rate brain and a strong stomach. You should at least try."

She was now looking really horrified, her eyes wider than I'd ever seen them. "But Edith, it would be the worst trick in the world to…to leave you here like that!"

"Well, I hope you'll at least give me a few lessons in dragon keeping before you disappear. I know I'm a magical being and all that, but it would help to be shown around a bit."

"Edith, stop it!"

"No," I said, quite firmly. "I won't stop it. The person who is going to stop it, is you. You're going to stop mooning about like the Lady of Shalott and get out of your tower and go down to Camelot yourself. I never did understand why she stayed in there weaving night and day and why she died. It's utter nonsense."

It was I who was speaking utter nonsense, but Gwendolyn was listening now and I felt I had a chance to make her see things differently for once.

"I wouldn't do it, and neither will you," I went on. "And I won't be the curse that fell, I won't be the Fall of the House of Worms or anything else so ridiculously gothic. Neither of us will. We'll be something quite different. I'll put this estate back on its feet and you'll go study medicine and when you come back you'll be able to find out why I can cure dragon bites and we'll bottle it up somehow and sell it or something and make a mint and rebuild everything. Dr. Worms' Dragon Pills has a nice ring."

I admit I ended a trifle weakly, but I felt I had conveyed my main points.

"Edith, what are you trying to do?" Her voice was slightly rough with emotion.

"You dear silly goose," I said, taking her by the shoulders and giving her an affectionate little shake. "I'm trying to give you permission to leave."

Then Gwendolyn put her head on my shoulder and cried. She was taller than me, but she felt oddly fragile now in my arms. I had never seen her cry before.

My heart was hurting me oddly. I thought of Mother's warning to me: *Edith, when one takes one's heart out of a box, one must be aware that it may be hurt.*

What had Gwendolyn said to me once? That her friendship might come at a cost?

I had told Gwendolyn to count the cost of her decision to stay here and guard the Abbey. But had I done that? Could I even begin?

Greater love hath no man than this, that a man lay down his life for a friend. Perhaps this pain in my heart was what that felt like, the kind of love that made someone take their friend's place willingly.

Gwendolyn had found no joy guarding the Abbey out of fear, but perhaps I would by doing it out of love.

And I knew all at once that Wormwood Abbey would not be a place of human sacrifice any longer, because by taking Gwendolyn's place willingly, I had broken that curse.

I was getting quite good at breaking curses.

A little later, after we'd gone through several handkerchiefs, Gwendolyn started to talk again. She told me how afraid she was that she wasn't clever enough (I told her she was). She demanded to know if I had thought about what I was giving up for her (I had: gas lighting, modern plumbing, and the occasional night at the theatre when a touring company came to town).

She laughed a bit then. "Now, I'm not agreeing to this mad plan of yours, I want you to know. I'm just thinking about it."

"Of course. That's because you're a sensible person," I said.

"But Edith, there must be something. A young man you like, or what about your work? Whatever it is that you go and write? It's a translation of something—something important, isn't it?"

"Oh, yes, it's terribly important." I said this without irony. I had seen that my stories brought hope to people in hopeless places. And that was indeed important. "But I've found I can write it just as well by candlelight as gas. And if I can defy Miss Binstead, who tries to get me on the Orphan Committee every single year, then I can defy any number of dragons to continue to write it."

"Perhaps one day you'll let me read it."

"Perhaps," I said. I didn't feel I could manage any more revelations just now. "For now, let's go join the family."

It was while we were all dining together that Mother dropped her own little bombshell.

"Well," said Mother, smiling sweetly as she took a sip of soup. "Really we mustn't complain about the wet roads, since I suppose it was all down to Saint George."

Gwendolyn and I both stared at her and I dropped my

soup spoon like a ninny, startling Francis who was sitting on the back of my chair.

"What was that, Mother?" I asked.

"Why, your Father and brother's name day, of course! I was saying, I suppose your father's namesake wanted us to celebrate his feast day here at Wormwood Abbey before we went home. Happy St. George's Day, everyone."

Gwendolyn and I looked at each other, remembering a bit of chainmail hidden in a jewelled casket. I was no papist, but at that moment it seemed quite natural to believe in Saint George's influence over recent events.

Father smiled at her as if they were sharing a private joke. "Thank you, Emily. I don't think I could choose a better place to mark that feast day. Perhaps we can make a family custom of celebrating it here. And then of course, there's always Michaelmas. That would also be very appropriate. Yes, I think we will have to come back quite soon to check on the estate. And I suspect George would be very glad to see the place during 'the Season,' as I believe it's called."

My heart warmed. Gwendolyn's eyes were shining a little. I'd seen that look of hope once before, but it had been quickly crushed. I prayed that this time, her hope would not be deferred.

I looked out the window and saw that Drake and Pilot were there on the terrace, looking out over the fells. Gwendolyn gave me a look and inclined her head towards the window. She seemed to be urging me to go out and talk to him.

I held out my arm to Francis. He jumped on to it. I was about to take him out with me when I remembered his previous reactions to Pilot. I held him out to George, who opened his eyes wide and held out his hand to him. Francis ran up his arm and settled in the space between George's collar and the back of his neck. George flushed with surprise and happiness.

As I passed his chair, I ruffled George's hair with my hand. It was a small gesture, but one I couldn't remember having done before.

Digging up one's heart, it turned out, had all sorts of unexpected consequences.

"Did you want to speak to me?" I said as I walked up to Drake, bending down to greet Pilot. My aversion to the man was entirely gone. I had thoroughly misjudged him and now felt that events had shown that his would be a friendship to be prized.

"Miss Worms. Yes, I did."

He smiled at me, and the sweetness of his smile no longer surprised me, though it still pleased. At this moment there was an eagerness about him, unfettered by shyness, that I hadn't seen before.

He handed me a letter, addressed to me. "This is from someone who'd very much like to meet you."

The writing was unusually beautiful, piquing my interest immediately. I opened it and scanned to the end to see the sender.

Helena Drake. I felt an odd shiver of anticipation. It recalled the feeling that I'd had of something drawing me to the house in the Faerie wood.

"You have something in common."

I looked up at him curiously. His dark eyes were warm and grave at the same time. As always, he seemed to be telling me more with them than with his words. And then he said the last thing in the world I expected him to say.

"You are both Marsi."

Edith and her friends, family, and dragons will return for
more mystery, adventure, and tea in
DRAKE HALL
Book 2 of *The Secrets of Ormdale*

———

Want to keep up with all the gossip from Ormdale? Go to
www.christinabaehr.com to subscribe to Christina's
newsletter!

ABOUT THE AUTHOR

Christina Baehr has a ridiculous number of children and lives on a hilltop in Tasmania also inhabited by poisonous snakes, which fortunately hibernate for much of the year.

Christina drank her first cup of coffee at age 41 which must have been what she had been missing her whole life because that was the same year she wrote her first novel, WORMWOOD ABBEY, and began her five book series *The Secrets of Ormdale.*

Christina is also a harpist, singer, and composer, and drinks a lot of tea.

www.christinabaehr.com

ACKNOWLEDGMENTS

First of all, a huge thanks to my creative and optimistic family for not telling me I was insane when I started furiously writing my first novel during Christmas while we all had stomach flu…even though insane I clearly was. Your enthusiasm, joy, and patience is amazing. I do not deserve you.

Secondly, Shiloh Longbottom's art has brought Edith, Francis, and the Abbey to luminous life, and brings me so much delight. I can't wait to see more of Ormdale through your eyes.

Two outstanding humans acted as book midwives for my debut novel.

One, my dear, faithful friend Suzannah, patiently coached me through the entire business of polishing and publishing a novel, including long texting sessions during at least one meltdown. And two, my newer dear friend, Wendee, spent hours formatting my first book for me, and encourages me by always liking my dodgy first drafts.

Thanks to beta reader Claire Trella Hill, who took time off promoting her debut novel to give me extremely valuable feedback. Because of you, Francis is a proper character.

Thanks to Isaac Lee for building me a lovely website and reacting with good humour to all of my technological freak-outs as I keyboard-mashed my way through editing the site, and for believing that I had it in me to be a successful author from the first time you heard I'd written a novel.

Thank you to all the ARC readers who jumped into Ormdale with heart-warming enthusiasm and helped me with hunting down the dreaded typos: you are better than dragon-slayers.

And finally, thank you to the extraordinary, magical creatures that are indie authors: many of you welcomed me with open arms, reviewing and promoting my book out of sheer kindness, especially Jacquelyn Benson, Claire Trella Hill, Rabia Gale, W.R. Gingell, Tara Grayce, Melissa McShane, Rosalie Oaks, Suzannah Rowntree, and Kate Stradling. Your graciousness and generosity has astonished me.

A NOTE ON THE DRAGONS

When I first had the idea for a family of secret dragon keepers in England in 1899, I knew that I didn't want to make up the dragons. I am lifelong reader of history, so the dragons had to be real ones.

For historical sources, I turned to Yorkshire legends and antiquarian sources of dragon lore. Then I stumbled across an obscure bestiary by an Elizabethan naturalist and folklorist, published in 1608. It turned out to be a gold mine (hoard?).

Thus, from Edward Topsell I have taken most of my knowledge of the typical habits of dragons. For example, that dragons emerge under a full moon, that they hibernate, their dietary peculiarities, and that there existed a kind of people called Marsi who can heal dragon bites with their saliva.

You'll find out even more about Marsi and historical dragons in the next book. (If you don't want to wait, you can find Topsell's original books at archive.org)

As for salamanders, I have visited the castle of Chambord in France which King Francois I embellished liberally with his personal motif. I am indebted to Martin Johnson for his article identifying Francois's salamander with the Sri Lankan water monitor lizard, *varanus salvator*.

Robert Knox was a real-life memoirist who encountered this creature during his time in Ceylon (modern day Sri Lanka). He asserted, along with Rivers, that they do not have venom, but recent research on the species has called that strongly into question.

Edith's mysterious pet, Francis, exhibits characteristics of both the living varanids (which are sometimes really kept as domestic animals today) and the legends of the extinct fire salamander. The amphibian we call a salamander today is quite a different animal, although it does secrete a toxic substance via its skin, in common with the legendary salamander.

The wyvern is a famous creature of legend. People disagree whether it qualifies as a dragon or not. I find it fascinating that only recently have palaeontologists confirmed that some ancient reptiles had feathers. Please note that the wyvern has *always* been depicted as a reptile with feathers.

Leaving dragons aside for a moment, I've tried to make all of my details about life in the Yorkshire Dales in 1899 as close as I possibly can to historical life. And St. George's Day in 1899 really did occur under a full moon.

AN EXCERPT FROM DRAKE HALL

Book 2 of *The Secrets of Ormdale*

Coming in January 2024

I was a little late, but still I paused to take a breath outside the door. Crossing the threshold of this room always felt like passing into another world; or another time.

It was not wholly an illusion. The hands of the large clock which stood next to me in the passage were still, the pendulum motionless. I suspected they had slept like that for years.

A voice came from inside the room. "Edith?"

My hand fluttered up in a habitual but futile attempt to tidy my ridiculous hair. I reminded myself that it never did any good, and opened the door.

The woman who sat in the bed always surprised me, no matter how many times I visited her. Her skin was milky pale and her hair was a heavy, waving auburn, with no traces yet of grey.

She was a queen receiving courtiers; her carved and curtained bed was a throne. As always, she wore a loose silk gown just such as the ones that Pre-Raphaelite enchantresses did; today it was the shade of an overcast sky.

Helena Drake was also wearing a smile of gentle amusement. "You are late."

"I saw the most extraordinary thing," I said, sitting in my accustomed chair. "A kind of river dragon, I think. Laying eggs in the bank of the river, near the Falls. Look, I've marked the place."

I held out to her my little notebook. This notebook had been left with me by my brother George, with strict instructions as to the kind of observations I must make about all the dragon species that lived in the Dale. I couldn't be expected to keep it as well as he would, of course, but until he returned to spend the summer holidays with us, the notebook would have to put up with me.

George had drawn up a rudimentary map of the Dale for me to mark sightings. This was the page I showed Helena now. She examined it carefully through a lorgnette which she wore on a chain around her neck.

"Ah, yes, I've seen this one many times. But you should have the place marked as 'Foss' not Falls. That is the old Norse word that is used in these parts. And that one has a name, you know."

"Oh?"

"Yes. It is known as Bess's Foss."

"Is it for any special Bess?"

"A very special Bess indeed," she said, with a look of meaning.

"You don't mean…" I trailed off.

Helena's son had told me that Queen Elizabeth I herself had bestowed this land on his ancestor in recognition of services rendered, though he had been vague about what those services were.

"Yes, I do," Helena answered simply.

"Did she come here?"

Helena nodded. "There is a bedroom here, and even a bed, in which she is supposed to have slept."

"Good heavens!"

At this point there was a soft knock at the door and the Drakes' butler came in with a small animal, which he placed in Helena's arms.

"Thank you, Forrester. I hope Mr. Darcy was quiet and good for his bath." Forrester bowed and left noiselessly. The man always reminded me of a shadow.

Helena looked after him for moment with softened eyes. "Mr Darcy bit him once, and poor Forrester wouldn't let anyone tell me about it for a whole day. I was furious when I found out. But it wasn't too late, thank God."

Like Gwendolyn, Helena had lost many people close to her. No wonder she was attached to this faithful retainer.

Helena stroked the creature tenderly. It was the general shape and size of a Pekinese dog. But it had colourful scales instead of fur, and small useless wings halfway down its body. It always seemed to me to have an expression of simmering fury. I had schooled myself not to stare at it, lest I annoy it further, but today I thought it looked if possible even more sour-tempered—no doubt the result of its involuntary ablutions.

"Ma'am, I've been meaning to ask. What was it exactly that the original Drake did to receive these lands? Why so close to the Abbey of my family?"

"I shall answer your question, Edith. On one condition." She carefully adjusted her lapdragon's collar.

"Yes?"

"That you will answer mine. What are your intentions?" There was a humorous quirk to her lips as she said this.

"My…intentions, ma'am?" I tried to imagine what she might be talking about.

Her eyes locked with mine. They were a striking grey, made more striking by the shade of her gown.

"Your intentions. Towards my son."

I blushed and burst into a nervous laugh.

"Really, ma'am! What have I done to deserve such an interrogation?"

"You must know that you are the first young woman whom Simon hasn't looked upon as a sister."

Despite her bantering tone, I could see she was in earnest.

I sobered. "I suppose I am."

"Well? What do you intend to do?" She tilted her head to one side and waited for my response.

"I can't help thinking I have rather an unfair advantage," I said, stalling, and trying to keep my tone light. "Perhaps Simon should be given the chance to compare me with other women who are also not his sisters, lest he make a hasty choice."

"Unfair advantage? Pshaw! We women must take all the advantages we can. We get so few of them. I for one will never fault you for pressing your advantage."

She then began to speak of other things but my heart was beating quickly and I did not follow them. Helena had as good as told me that Simon was infatuated with me, and that I should press in for the kill, so to speak. This was a most extraordinary conversation to have with a young man's mother.

But then, I'd never had an ordinary conversation with Helena Drake. From the first time I had come to see her, this had been so. She was quite unlike anyone I had ever encountered. Perhaps she *was* an enchantress, and I her acolyte. I could not believe that *I* was magical, despite my newfound ability to heal dragon bites, but I could easily believe it of her. There was something about her, and about this house, that belonged more to the fairy books my stepmother had read to me than the England I thought I knew.

A thought sparked in my mind. "Ma'am, you said you would answer my question."

Now she eyed me with a touch of respect. "Well done, Edith. I thought you'd let it slip by."

I felt a glow of pleasure at her praise. She went on. "Bartholomew Drake was granted these lands as a gift because whilst on a voyage with his uncle, Sir Francis Drake, he was responsible for the acquisition of a Spanish galleon containing, among other treasures, a rare young dragon of a species found only in the New World."

I sucked in a breath. "Of course! They sent him here because the Worm Wardens were already here, at the Abbey. And what happened to the dragon? Do you know?"

"I believe it retreated to the caves and it was that which gave Bartholomew Drake the idea of concealing his treasure there. The old legend of dragons guarding gold, you know."

"Yes! His pirate loot. Good gracious, it's like something out of Stevenson, isn't it?"

"We prefer 'privateer', my dear," she said. It was a gentle reproof, but a real one.

"Oh. Of course."

"So now tell me, what is it that makes Ormdale particularly special ?"

"You mean besides the presence of dragons and pi— privateers in the middle of Yorkshire sheepland?" I asked.

She nodded.

"Well," I said, lacing my fingers together thoughtfully. "Ormdale already had a respectable population of native dragons, going back to the Middle Ages. And then you told me one of my ancestors was associated with the East India Company and collected Oriental dragons, presumably including an ancestor of your Mr. Darcy, and now you tell me we had at least one American dragon in the 1500s. So I suppose we're a bit of a dragon menagerie. A zoological gardens, if you will, like the Rothschilds' new museum at Tring, except for mythical beasts."

"Hardly mythical," she murmured in faint protest.

There was a pause, in which I realised that Helena had pointedly stopped telling me about family history. Helena's silences were always as important as her speeches.

"There's something else, isn't there? Something I missed," I admitted at last, looking up a little ruefully. "Something important."

Helena smiled at me. "But you haven't missed it. It's somewhere in your mind. You'll find it, later."

"But ma'am, I wonder if you would tell me about an ancestor of mine I've heard stories of? A woman who drove about with a monkey?"

"Ah yes, Lady Amelia. She was married to Sir Anthony, the East India Company gentleman. He was knighted during the Regency. I knew their son, Barnaby. He was an old man, of course, by then. He it was who built the glasshouse at the Abbey as a home for the exotic dragons from the subcontinent. I believe he spent all of his father's money in a few decades, just in building and heating it. But he loved them, you know."

Her eyes had grown unfocused, as if she was entering into a memory fully. And then I thought that tears came to her eyes for an instant.

She smiled at me suddenly, the moment gone. "Well, now. Shall we read?"

This was always part of our routine. Helena would pick up whatever novel she was currently reading, and I would take one from my pocket or choose one from her shelves, and we would read in companionable silence until it was time for me to go back to the Abbey for tea.

It felt odd at first, but I grew to enjoy it. Helena's illness did not spare her much energy for movement or even conversation. Sitting quietly together was a way that she could enjoy companionship without being drained. I felt privileged to provide it.

In conversation I felt a little awed by her, and found myself longing to please her. But in these quiet hours we seemed to settle wordlessly into a kind of comfortable equality. We were, in these moments, no longer mentor and pupil, but simply fellow readers.

I glanced at the volumes already lying on the small table next to me. The outlandish title of one of them sounded a faint note in my mind. *The Mabinogion.* What was it? Something my father had mentioned? I picked it up and read this on the first page:

In the centre of the chamber King Arthur sat upon a seat of green rushes, over which was spread a covering of flame-coloured satin, and a cushion of red satin was under his elbow.

"I wonder where they got all that satin," I murmured. I then spent a happy hour immersed in these Welsh tales of enchanted glades and mountains, auburn-haired beauties, Arthurian knights with unfathomable Welsh names, and mysterious beasts that assisted them on their adventures.

Then I said goodbye to Helena and showed myself out. I was relieved that I did not run into Simon on this visit.

After his mother's surprising instructions to 'reel him in' I did not think I could face him until I had had a little time to reflect.

Our friendship had begun inauspiciously. I had judged him untrustworthy at first sight. His manner and physical appearance (tall, dark, and well-made) marked him as the Byronic hero of a gothic novel. Not at all the kind of young man I intended to marry—if marry I ever did, which I was not at all sure I would. Gothic men, I thought, did not often make good husbands—at least if literature was to be believed on this point.

Instead, I had found him to be kind, humble, and given to unexpected laughter. To be sure, he was a little stilted and old-fashioned in his manners, but that was only to be expected given his upbringing in remote Ormdale. He had won my liking, but not my heart.

As I crossed the river on my way back to the Abbey, I looked back at Drake Hall, glimpsing its elegant Elizabethan lines through the green, whispering trees. It was a very lovely place indeed. And Drake, I had discovered, was a very good man.

In the last two months I had discovered a new family, a new home, and new roles which I must try to fill. I was a born healer of dragon poisons. And I was learning to be a dragon keeper. I was even, for the first time in my life, really learning how to be a friend to someone—and if anyone needed a friend, my cousin Gwendolyn certainly did.

I was still finding my footing in this extraordinary place that had suddenly become mine. Now was not the time to lose my head over a man for the first time. A love affair was quite out of the question. The very idea tired me.

Simon would have to master his feelings for me. I comforted myself by telling me they were probably nothing more than those which usually accompanied a boy's first infatuation.

I turned away from the hidden valley and climbed up the path to the Abbey.

"It's Whitsunday Eve, Gwendolyn," I said.

"Oh, yes," my cousin responded absently.

"Mother will be arranging flowers for the altar," I continued, mostly to myself as Gwendolyn was preoccupied. "I usually change the altar cloth and candles. They're always red for Whitsunday, you know."

This was a day I usually spent in ecclesiastical activities appropriate to the dutiful daughter of a clergyman.

I had never before spent it in wiggling a dead rat on a string in the direction of a hungry wyvern. (A wyvern, by the way, is a two-legged winged dragon, both scaled and feathered, about the size of the large Alpine dogs of St. Bernard.)

I had, of course, questioned my cousin Gwendolyn as to the reason behind this ritual the first time we had performed it, some weeks ago.

"Oh," she had said reflectively, "I suppose it's because the wyvern doesn't like to eat dead things."

This had sounded the most reasonable thing in the world. Which worried me a little. Really, the most odd things were becoming commonplace, while everyday things had begun to feel strange.

"Well," I had replied. "I myself prefer to eat dead things. Though it sounds rather macabre when you put it that way, doesn't it?"

Today, however, on the Eve of Whitsunday, I considered myself an old hand at feeding mythical beasts deep in the bowels of my family's gothic ancestral home. Perhaps this really was something I was born to do.

I had spent the last month learning about some of the mysterious objects in the Muniments Room and helping Gwendolyn with any dragon handling tasks that popped up. Now we were getting to the part of the year when the creatures would come out in earnest. It wouldn't just be one lonely wyvern roused from hibernation too early in the year.

I wasn't yet clear exactly how many species of dragon existed in this Yorkshire valley, especially given yesterday's conversation with Helena. I expected to find out soon. I wondered whether I was up to the job.

Gwendolyn was sitting on a stool outside the cell I was in with the wyvern, making some notes in a book by the dim light of lantern on a hook. She was paying little or no attention to me, which I took as generally a good sign.

"Passive indicative!" I called out to test her, while I continued my grim puppetry.

Gwendolyn didn't hesitate. "*Amor, amaris, amatur...*" She chanted the conjugations quite musically from memory, without a complaint.

"Good. Now Greek."

This elicited a very slight groan. Gwendolyn had done surprisingly well in her Latin studies, to which she credited the childhood French her otherwise useless governess had insisted upon. Unfortunately, she made up for her aptitude for Latin with an inexorable dislike of Greek.

Still, we persisted. Gwendolyn would need a basic knowledge of both ancient languages to successfully sit the entrance examination at the London Medical School for Women, as she hoped to do before the year was out.

The wyvern was watching the stiff rodent jerk about with what I felt sure was suspicion. I tried to make it lively, but the wyvern's bright eye began to look more intrigued by my own gyrations than its dinner.

Suddenly I heard a man's voice call down from the top of the stair that led into the cellars where the holding cells for wayward dragons were located, and which we presently occupied. I couldn't help jumping a little in surprise.

"Miss Worms? It's Alfred. May I come down?" The voice was slow and solid, and deeply of the Dale.

"Yes, yes, please do," called Gwendolyn.

With a snap of the wyvern's powerful jaw the rodent was gone. My jolt of surprise must have lent verisimilitude to the corpse's animation.

"Ah," I sighed and withdrew from the cell, shutting the cell door behind me, relieved to conclude the daily *danse macabre*.

Alfred Dugdale, our new estate Manager, came down the stairs with a heavy tread. He was about forty-five and as solid and expressionless as the Great Rock which stood in the dale. Part of me longed to see him surprised. But I reflected that if wyverns could not succeed in provoking a visible reaction from him, I did not wish to see what could.

"Shepherd's been to see me. Sheep's all safe in upland paddocks."

Alfred often spoke in this abbreviated way. His words, like his features, seemed chiseled in stone.

"Thank you, Dugdale," said Gwendolyn, making a note in her book.

I looked back and forth between them.

"Does that mean we can free the wyvern?" I asked.

"Well, that's a little dramatic, Edith," said Gwendolyn, shutting her book and standing up. "But yes, the lambs are no longer in the immediate vicinity, which will afford them sufficient protection."

I turned to Alfred. "The dragons don't like to go too far into the fells," I said knowingly. "Because of the cold and wind."

Alfred's face was still as a corpse. I thought that he, at least, need never fear being eaten by a Wyvern. The rat had more animation.

"But you knew that, being raised in the Dale," I ended weakly.

Despite his lack of small talk I was deeply grateful for his presence on the estate. Gwendolyn had been struggling to run it alone since the sudden death of her father and brother at the end of winter.

Alfred was some sort of cousin to the small family of servants that lived and worked at the Abbey. Because he'd been born and raised in Ormdale, he was aware that the Dale was home to England's last surviving dragons, and that we, the Worms family, were England's last surviving dragon keepers.

He got on well with the shepherds and tenant farmers on our estate and had some new ideas for making the estate financially profitable, something it seemed my ancestors had not bothered much about. He'd lived outside of the Dale for a time, working as a supervisor at the big lime-works in Swallowdale, and I hoped this would give him a fresh perspective on how to solve the estate's pecuniary problems. Sometimes his ideas were a little too fresh for Gwendolyn, who seemed to have cast herself in the role of gatekeeper and preserver of the family traditions.

Gwendolyn and I had next to lead the wyvern up the stairs, down a passage, into the kitchen and from thence into the kitchen yard. It turned out to be much easier than I expected as the wyvern seemed quite happy to simply follow me.

"Why do you think I had you feed it, Edith?" said Gwendolyn, when I remarked on this.

Once in the yard I carefully removed its collar, admiring the revelation of iridescent scales in sunlight.

The gate to the walled kitchen yard was open and I expected it to bolt. Instead, it settled down in the dusty yard like a chicken sunning itself.

A gigantic scaly chicken, with a murderous looking barb on the end of its tail.

"Gwendolyn. It's not going anywhere," I said in a low tone after a moment or two.

"You fed it too much," she accused. "It doesn't want to find its own food now. It knows a good thing when it sees it," she said this with distaste, as if the creature was morally culpable for its lack of enterprise.

Just at that moment a flock of birds flew over the kitchen yard, not much higher than our heads. I was hardly aware they were there before the Wyvern stood up, lifted its head and opened its jaws extremely wide, with a bizarre ingressive honk that reminded me strongly of the time my brother George had croup.

What happened next was even more startling. Half a dozen or so of the birds dropped straight into the creature's mouth, as if they'd been sucked out of the sky. The Wyvern then snapped its jaws shut and settled down to bask again at our feet.

I was speechless for a moment.

"I don't think I've been feeding it enough."

"Greedy," sniffed Gwendolyn.

"Is it going to live here now? Just outside the kitchen? Won't it make the servants nervous?"

"Edith, the servants are as used to seeing dragons as I am, and a sight more than you are. Besides, it's breeding season now and it will be looking for it's mate. Oh, no!" she exclaimed, voice was full of dread.

"What?" I asked, swinging round to look about me, expecting some alarming creature had made an appearance.

"It's just…you do know about…*all that*, don't you?" Gwendolyn's voice sounded pinched.

She looked so stricken that I quickly guessed what she was talking about. I burst out laughing.

"Oh, Gwen. You do remember that I'm a clergyman's daughter, don't you?"

Gwendolyn blinked at me.

"It's like this," I said, reassuringly linking my arm through hers and walking back towards the kitchen. "Ever since I can remember, people have been coming to father to confess things," I explained. "I mean, they don't tell me, of course, but one soon figures out quite a lot, especially when it's young girls not much older than oneself. And Mother's always been wonderfully honest with me about *all that*, as you call it."

Gwendolyn looked at me with respect as we stepped into the big kitchen. "Edith. Whenever I think you can't surprise me anymore, you come out with something like that."

I shrugged. "Let's have a cup of tea. You're nervous about Monday, aren't you?"

My particular pet dragon, Francis, saw me as soon as I came into the room. He left his warm spot by the kitchen range to climb deftly up my dress to his customary place on my shoulder.

"Of course I'm nervous! I'm sure Dr Worthing is going to send me packing."

"Well, he'll have to listen to you first. You've made an appointment."

There was a homely teapot on the kitchen table, steaming appealingly. It was most likely intended for us, but one didn't like to make assumptions with these servants, who were the descendants of vikings. One didn't like to imagine what they might do if really provoked.

"Cook, might I steal a cup or two?"

Martha, our Cook, waved a hand at me. She wasn't much for niceties, and was currently at the chopping block, cutting up a carcass with grim enthusiasm.

I found two cups and poured out while Gwendolyn sat at the table.

"Have I been very horrible?" said Gwendolyn, clasping her cup and looking up at me with her beautiful eyes. Now that I knew my cousin better, I found Gwendolyn's mixture of imperious authority and childlike vulnerability rather endearing. I was no longer intimidated by her air of aristocracy, knowing it disguised her own deep-seated feelings of inferiority.

"You've been a little terse," I admitted. "Have you given any thought to Alfred's proposal for the limeworks?"

Gwendolyn looked guilty.

"Father would have never entertained the thought for a moment. He was totally against any kind of excavation."

I considered this for moment.

"Gwendolyn, your father ran the estate his way for twenty years. And it didn't turn out very well. Why not try your way?"

"And what is my way, Edith?" She set her tea cup down with an exasperated click.

"I don't know. But while you are sorting that out we might try Alfred's. My father hired him in large part so that you could focus on other things," I reminded her gently.

"Simon says the same thing," she snorted.

"I have the greatest respect for Simon's opinion," I smiled, tickling Francis's throat absently.

"Do you? Is that all?" She looked at me sideways as she sipped her tea.

"Is what all?"

"Respect. For Simon."

I glanced at Martha. The kitchen was very large, and she was on the other side of it, thwacking through flesh and bone.

"Is he here today?" I asked.

"He left after I called him a dunderhead. I told you I was being horrible. Anyway, he doesn't mind. He's had to bear with my moods since he was four. He's a perfect lamb about it. You…you will be kind to him, won't you? Whatever happens? He deserves a little kindness."

"Well, I won't call him a dunderhead," I retorted. And she laughed.

Gwendolyn didn't laugh often, but it always felt like striking gold when she did. I had stayed at the Abbey at first for my cousin's sake. At moments like this, I felt a glow of conviction that whatever precisely the nature of my role here turned out to be, I had made the right choice in staying, at least for now. I had never had a friend of my own age before, and our friendship was a source of great pleasure to me.

I glanced out the window into the kitchen yard. I was pleased to see it was empty. The wyvern had gone in search of its mate.